Sinéad MORIARTY

Finding Hope

Gill Books

Gill Books
Hume Avenue
Park West
Dublin 12
www.gillbooks.ie

Gill Books is an imprint of M.H. Gill and Co.

978 07171 95220

Design and print origination by O'K Graphic Design, Dublin
Edited by Esther Ní Dhonnacha
Printed and bound in Lithuania by ScandBook AB
This book is typeset in 12 on 17pt Garamond Premiere Pro.

The paper used in this book comes from the wood pulp of sustainably managed forests.

5 4 3 2 1

For all children.

*Don't ever forget that you are never too small
to make a difference.*

'Once we start to act, hope is everywhere.'
–Greta Thunberg

CHAPTER 1

The last Friday in September was the day things changed for Hope. She didn't realise it at first. It took her a little while to understand.

It started out as just another boring day at school when, after lunch, Mrs Lannigan said she was going to show them a TED talk.

'Oh no,' Katie whispered. 'Not another boring talk about education or creativity.'

'Or how "fun" maths can be,' Jayne said, groaning.

Hope grinned at them but said nothing. She actually quite liked TED talks, but she'd never admit it. Her two best friends thought they were dead boring, so Hope pretended she did too.

1

She'd been pretending a lot in the last year. She pretended that she didn't cry herself to sleep every night. She pretended that she didn't miss her mum every single day. She pretended that she didn't feel jealous of her friends having their mums picking them up at the school gate, while she walked home alone. She pretended that she liked having pasta and burgers every night, because Dad was a rubbish cook. She pretended that she didn't hate that Dad was going out on dates with Rebecca's mum; Rebecca, who was the one girl in her class she really didn't like. She pretended that she was 'just fine', when inside she felt lonely, heartbroken and lost.

Poppy and Daisy had each other. Her twin sisters were connected as if by an invisible thread. Hope often heard them talking late into the night through her bedroom wall. She wished that she had a twin, someone to talk to when she lay awake at night unable to fall asleep. Someone to talk to about Mum and how unfair it was that she had died so suddenly, after only being sick for five weeks. Ovarian cancer, diagnosed too late, too advanced to treat. Hope longed for someone to help her make sense of the world.

She couldn't talk to Dad because he was heartbroken too, and tired and stressed. He was trying to be a dad *and* a mum, rushing home from work to cook and help with their homework. But then, a few weeks ago, he had started going out on Fridays and leaving the twins in charge at home. They were fifteen and supposed to be responsible enough to look after Hope, but they basically just ignored her and watched YouTube, scrolled through TikTok and Snapchat, painted their nails and practised doing smoky eyes on each other. Whenever Hope tried to join in, they told her she was 'too young for make-up and social media'. It was only a week ago that Hope had found out where Dad had been going on Friday nights. She had thought that he was meeting up with his best friend, Dave, but then she heard the twins talking about 'Dad's new girlfriend'.

Hope had felt sick. How could Dad have a girlfriend already? What about Mum? Then again, Mum had been dead for nearly a year and Dad *was* lonely. But still, the thought of him going out with another woman felt all wrong.

And when Hope had found out who the new girlfriend was, well, that made it *so* much worse. She had heard Daisy say, 'Isn't Janice Rebecca Harte's mother?'

'Yeah,' Poppy had replied. 'She got divorced a while ago and apparently Dad met her at some school meeting for Hope's class and they got chatting.'

Hope had had to cover her mouth because she was afraid that she might actually be sick. Rebecca Harte was the most spoilt, annoying, selfish, mean girl in the class. How could her lovely dad be dating Rebecca's mother? It was all wrong. Everything was wrong.

So, on that September day, sitting in the classroom, Hope was feeling very sorry for herself. But when Mrs Lannigan put on the TED talk, everything changed.

The minute she heard Greta Thunberg talking about climate change, Hope was hooked. Not just interested, but totally mesmerised. It was the first time Hope didn't have to pretend to be interested in something since Mum had died. She'd been faking interest in sports and school, but really she was just stumbling through the days, missing Mum so badly. But now ... it was as if Greta was speaking to her directly.

Hope even managed to block out Rebecca's annoying voice. 'OMG, what a total nerd. What teenager has dorky plaits like that? She obviously has no friends and decided to bore us all about climate change instead.'

Hope heard the other girls giggling about the fact that Greta said she had stopped talking when she was eleven. She wished Rebecca would take a leaf out of Greta's book and shut up and let her listen.

Hope blocked all the chatter out and hung on every single word Greta said. This girl had a mission. A passion. Hope wanted to be like her. She missed feeling excited and interested in things. Since Mum died, she had just felt numb all the time. But Greta Thunberg was full of passion: she knew what she wanted, and what she wanted was to save the planet.

While her classmates yawned and whispered to each other, Hope listened like she'd never listened before. She soaked in every word.

Mum had told them about Greta Thunberg and tried to explain about climate change and global warming and the plastic in the oceans harming the fish and how you should turn off your lights and stuff, but the twins had said they were happy it was getting warmer and they didn't eat fish anyway, so who cared? Hope had giggled and Mum had rolled her eyes and sighed.

But here was this girl explaining it all so clearly, telling Hope about the world and how bad things had got, how fossil fuel emissions were destroying the whole planet – it reminded Hope of Mum.

Hope wasn't sure what fossil fuels were, exactly, or what emissions meant, but she'd google them when she got home. And she was horrified to hear that two hundred species were going extinct every single day – that was crazy. There'd be no animals left if this kept going!

Hope needed to focus on something that mattered. Since Mum died, she'd felt really lost, but now it was as if Mum was speaking to her through Greta. Climate change was something Mum had told her about, something she had tried to get her children to care about. Mum had wanted to make the world a better place, but they hadn't listened to her. Now Hope wanted to listen and learn and do something positive. It would make her feel close to Mum and distract her mind from being sad all the time. So she decided, there and then, that she was going to help Greta Thunberg to save the planet.

She wasn't sure how, but she was going to try.

CHAPTER 2

D ad stood in front of the mirror fixing his shirt. It was his best shirt. The one he'd worn out to Mum's birthday dinner last year.

She'd been forty-one. She'd died just six weeks later. When Hope had helped zip up her mum's favourite dress that day, she had never ever imagined that it would be Mum's last birthday. Mum had looked so beautiful and so happy. Mum and Dad didn't usually go to fancy restaurants, but Dad was treating her. She had twirled around and Hope had clapped as the beautiful red silk material swished around her like a wave.

'Thanks for helping me get ready, Hope.' Mum had kissed her, leaving a red lipstick mark on her cheek.

'Muuuuum,' Hope had moaned, rubbing it off. Now she wished she hadn't. She wished she'd left it on her face forever. So that she would always have Mum's kiss on her cheek.

'Do I look older?' Mum had asked.

'You look beautiful,' Hope told her. And she did. So beautiful.

'Thank you, my lovely.' Mum had hugged her and Hope had inhaled her perfume. It was Mum's smell. Chanel's Coco Mademoiselle Eau de Parfum. Mum always said that her perfume was the only posh thing about her. 'I may not have money for fancy clothes, but I'll always smell posh,' she'd say, laughing.

Nowadays, Hope kept Mum's half-full bottle of Coco Mademoiselle perfume under her mattress and, when she was missing her very badly, she'd spray a tiny bit onto her pillow so she could feel Mum close by.

'Why are you wearing that shirt?' she asked her father accusingly.

Dad's cheeks went red. 'I'm, uhm, well, I'm going out to dinner, Hope.'

Hope's eyes narrowed. 'Who with?'

He paused, and then said, 'With a lady called Janice.'

Hope gasped. He must really like Rebecca's mum if he was wearing his special 'fancy birthday dinner shirt' out to meet her. That was his shirt for going out with Mum on special dates, not stupid old Janice. Hope's lower lip began to wobble.

Dad walked over and put his big strong arms around his youngest daughter. He held her tight.

'I haven't forgotten your mum, pet. I still miss her and think about her all the time. But life moves on and we have to do the same. Janice is just a nice lady I enjoy chatting with. I'm lonely, Hope, and it's nice to have another adult to talk to. We're only going out for dinner, it's all very casual. No one is going to replace Mum. OK?'

Hope nodded and snuggled against his chest, secretly hoping that her tears would mess up his shirt. She knew Dad was trying to reassure her, but she also knew that people got remarried. Her Uncle Frank had divorced her Auntie Grace and he'd got married to Denise two years ago. She knew that Dad had only met Janice a few weeks ago, but she was scared: scared that he'd fall in love with her and that Rebecca would end up being her stepsister. That would be the worst thing that could happen, ever.

Dad picked up his jacket, headed down the hall and popped his head into the TV room. 'Right, you two, look after your little sister and no fighting. I won't be late.'

Hope heard the twins say goodnight and, as her dad passed her in the hall, he planted a kiss on her forehead. 'Bed by ten, please,' he said.

Hope nodded, not having the slightest intention of going to bed until at least eleven. As he was closing the door, he said, 'I love you, Hope, don't ever forget that.'

'I love you too, Dad,' Hope whispered to the closed door, 'but don't you dare fall in love with Janice!'

Hope went into the TV room. The twins were taking selfies and pouting into their phones. They looked really dumb with their lips all puffed out.

'Dad said you're not to post any photos on Instagram,' Hope reminded them.

Daisy rolled her eyes. 'Dad doesn't understand social media.'

'He does. He says it's dangerous because bad men go on Instagram looking to be friends with young girls.'

Poppy burst out laughing. 'Dad is, like, a hundred years old and hasn't a clue about Instagram. He thinks everything is dangerous – Instagram, Snapchat, TikTok ... He's so over-protective, it's annoying.'

Poppy did have a point. Dad was a bit of a worrier, and since Mum had died, he'd been obsessed with trying to

10

be a good parent and keeping on top of things. But he was wasting his time with the twins. They'd always been a bit loose with the truth, but since Mum had died they lied all the time and did whatever they wanted. Dad hadn't a notion of half the things they got up to. Mum had been much more clued in. The twins ran rings around poor Dad.

'Do you want to watch *Friends*?' Daisy asked.

'Really? Yes.' Hope was delighted. Her sisters never wanted to do stuff with her.

'I'll microwave some popcorn.' Poppy got up and went into the kitchen.

This was great. A night snuggled up on the couch with her sisters, eating popcorn and watching *Friends*, would be so fun. Hope pulled her cosy blanket out from behind the couch and cuddled up.

Daisy put on Hope's favourite *Friends* episode – the one where no-one is ready to go to the fancy event at the museum and Ross is going nuts.

Poppy came back in with the popcorn and handed Hope the bowl.

Hope patted the couch. 'Come on, get comfy.'

The twins grinned at her. 'The thing is, Hope, we're actually going out. Jackson Daly is having people over to his house, and we knew Dad would say no because he thinks Jackson is a bit wild because he got suspended last week and all the adults in town are talking about it and making, like, a really big deal about it,' Daisy said.

Hope frowned. Dad was right: Jackson *was* wild. He'd been suspended for coming into school drunk.

'But Dad said you were to look after me,' Hope said, putting the popcorn bowl down, not feeling like eating anymore.

'I know, but we've put on your favourite TV show and made you popcorn, so what's the big deal? We'll be back in a couple of hours and if you have any emergency or whatever, you can call us,' Daisy said.

Hope had a Nokia phone that Dad had bought her after Mum died. He said the phone was only to be used if there was an emergency, or if she was feeling sad and wanted to talk to him. It wasn't a smartphone like she'd wanted. Dad said she was too young for an expensive phone like that.

Hope really, really didn't want to be left alone. She wanted to be with her sisters. She hated being in the house by herself. She felt scared and every little noise freaked her out.

'Don't go, please,' she begged.

Poppy put her hands on her hips. 'You're being kind of selfish now. We want to go and have some fun with our friends. It's been the worst year ever, and we need distractions. We thought you'd be cool about it, Hope.' The twins glared at her.

Hope sank back into the couch, holding her blanket up like a shield from their anger. *Was* she being selfish? Or were they being selfish leaving her on her own? It had been the worst year for her too. But it didn't matter what she thought; they always did what they wanted. It was two against one, so Hope was never going to win any arguments. The twins always stuck together.

'OK, fine. But don't come back late or Dad will find out and be furious and it won't be my fault.'

Daisy grinned. 'Don't worry about Dad, he'll be out later than us. He's taking Janice to La Cucina and whenever he went there with Mum they always stayed out for ages.'

What? La Cucina? That was Mum's favourite restaurant in town. How dare Dad take stupid Janice there in his best shirt? Hope wanted to cry now. This night just kept getting worse.

'Hey.' Poppy sat down and put her arm around her sister. 'Don't worry about Janice, Daisy and I will get rid of her if it gets serious. No one is going to replace Mum, ever.'

Hope smiled up at her sister. 'Good.' If the twins wanted to chase Janice away, the woman had no hope. Daisy and Poppy could be super scary. Hope felt a bit better.

'Come on,' Daisy said, tugging at her twin sister. 'We need to finish our make-up and get down to Jackson's ASAP.'

By the time Hope had finished watching her favourite episode of *Friends*, the twins had left for Jackson's party. The house seemed so quiet without them. Hope went into the kitchen to put away her popcorn bowl and get a drink of water. The wind howled outside the window and the trees swayed in the dark night. It was creepy. Hope went upstairs to her bedroom, where she felt safer.

She took out the two special photos of her mum that she kept in her bedside locker. Sometimes they were too painful for her to look at, but tonight she needed to see them. There was one of Mum holding her when she was a baby and one of her and Mum on Hope's tenth birthday. Mum was holding the birthday cake she'd made for her – it was a chocolate biscuit cake covered in Smarties. In the photo Mum was smiling at Hope with so much love that it made Hope's heart hurt. She missed Mum's love, she missed her smile. Hope kissed her mum's picture and put the photos back. Then she sprayed a tiny bit of Coco Mademoiselle on her pillow. The bottle was only a quarter full now, so she had to be really careful not to use too much so it would last.

Hope lay down on her pillow and sniffed. Mum. It smelt like Mum.

Hope must have nodded off, because the next thing she knew, the front door banged shut and she heard Dad whistling to himself. She sat bolt upright in her bed. She glanced at her clock. It was just past eleven.

She tiptoed across to the twins' room. It was empty; they must still be out. She snuck back to her room and texted them: **SOS – Dad is home!!!!!**

OMG, don't let him upstairs, Poppy texted back.

What am I supposed to do? Hope thought angrily. Not only had her sisters abandoned her, now they wanted her to keep it a secret as well?

Hope climbed wearily out of her bed again and went downstairs. She met her dad at the bottom of the steps.

'I was just coming up to check on you,' he said. 'Are the twins in their room?'

'Uhm, yes, yeah they are.' Hope tried to think of a way to keep him downstairs. 'Actually, Dad, I need to talk to you about something.'

'OK, that sounds serious,' Dad said.

'It is,' Hope replied, and she walked into the kitchen, hoping he'd follow her. Thankfully, he did. They sat down opposite each other at the kitchen table.

'What's up, love?' Dad asked.

Out of the corner of her eye, she saw the twins sneaking past the window.

Hope scrambled for something to say and then she remembered.

'What are fossil fuel emissions?'

Dad frowned. 'What?'

'We watched a TED talk by Greta Thunberg in school today and she was talking all about fossil fuel emissions ruining the world. But I don't know what they are and I meant to google it but then ... but then ...'

But then I saw you in your going-out shirt, and heard about the posh restaurant, and the date with Janice, and I got side-tracked, she thought darkly.

What she said was, 'But then I knew that you would be able to tell me what they are because you're so smart.'

Dad *was* smart – not super smart like Katie's dad, who was a pharmacist, or like Jayne's dad, who was a doctor – but smart in his own way. Dad was the manager of the big PowerCity store at the edge of the town where everyone went to get computers and fridges and washing machines and hoovers and everything else they needed.

Dad had had to leave school aged sixteen when his own dad died, and he'd had to get a job to help his mum support his three younger sisters. They all lived in America now. Auntie Jeanne had emigrated first and then the other two sisters had followed. Hope's gran had been lonely for her daughters, so she had gone to live there too.

Hope knew that her dad sometimes felt less smart than her friends' dads because he'd never finished school, but Mum always used to say that he was a better, kinder man than any of those college-educated husbands, and he had more common sense than all of them put together.

'I'll tell you what,' Dad said, 'let's google it together. I don't want to get it wrong and have Mrs Lannigan calling up and giving out to me.' He grinned at Hope and went to pick up the family laptop from where it lived on a small desk in the corner of the kitchen. He googled 'National Geographic Kids fossil fuels', and they bent over the screen together and read: 'Over the past 150 years, industrialised countries have been burning large amounts of fossil fuels such as oil and gas. The gases released into the atmosphere act like an invisible "blanket", trapping heat from the sun and warming the Earth. This is known as the "Greenhouse Effect".

So we need to stop using oil and gas, Hope thought. *That can't be so hard, can it?*

She put her hand on Dad's arm to keep his attention. 'How can we stop people using oil and gas? We have to save the planet, Dad. Mum tried to tell us about it, but we didn't listen. We have to act now.'

Dad rubbed his eyes. 'It's way past your bedtime, Hope. Can we talk about this in the morning?'

Hope had to stop him leaving the room. The twins wouldn't have changed out of their party clothes yet. 'NO! We have to sort this out now!'

He put his hands on his daughter's shoulders. 'Hope, we're not going to save the world tonight. I promise to do more research with you tomorrow. Come on now, let's get some sleep.'

Just as Hope was about to throw herself in front of the kitchen door to stop him heading out, it opened. The twins came in fake-yawning in their dressing gowns, with their clothes hidden underneath. Poppy's sparkly red top was peeping out. They still had their make-up and false eyelashes on, and Hope thought they looked ridiculous. Dad didn't seem to notice, though.

'Oh, hi Dad, did you have a good night?' Poppy yawned.

'Yes, thanks. Now come on, all of you, bed.'

'Yeah, I'm wrecked,' Daisy said, winking at Hope when Dad's head was turned.

They all went upstairs. Dad kissed them one by one, then went into his room. When his bedroom door was closed, the twins hugged Hope gratefully. 'Thanks, sis, you saved us,' Poppy said.

'You owe me,' Hope said.

'I'll teach you how to do a smoky eye, OK?' Daisy said.

'I'd prefer it if you helped me stop people using oil and gas.'

'What?'

'We have to stop the Greenhouse Effect.'

Daisy stared at her. 'OK, you're, like, speaking a different language now. What've you been watching?'

'Nothing. I just care about climate change,' Hope said.

'Oh my God, are you serious?'

'Yes, very.'

19

'You are *not* to turn into that Swedish girl with the plaits who makes all those boring speeches,' Poppy warned her. 'You're not allowed embarrass us.'

'Greta Thunberg is incredible, and at least she's trying to save the planet.'

Daisy rolled her eyes. 'Here we go, another of Hope's obsessions. We've had Malala Whatshername, and now it's Greta Thunhead.'

'Remember when Hope made us watch that boring film about the guy who just kept running all the time?' said Poppy.

'OMG, that was sooooo long and boring and what was the point?' Daisy groaned.

'*Forrest Gump* is a brilliant film! It's about being who you are and appreciating what you have and being a good person,' Hope said, sick to death of her sisters making fun of her and the people she admired.

'He just ran and ate chocolate. How is that remotely interesting?' Poppy said.

'And that blind ballet dancer you loved, Like, seriously, how mental do you have to be to take up ballet if you're blind?' Daisy rolled her eyes.

'Alicia Alonso was incredibly brave. She refused to let

her blindness stop her doing what she loved,' Hope hissed.

'How can you dance on stage, pirouetting about and not fall off? It's so dumb.'

Hope wanted to smack them both. They just didn't get it. They didn't see how amazing these people were – brave and brilliant. But as great as Hope thought they were, Greta was on a whole new level. Greta was trying to save the whole world.

She stormed off into her bedroom and slammed the door shut, leaving her sisters giggling outside. Mum had understood her. Mum thought Alicia Alonso was super brave. Mum had loved the movie *Forrest Gump*, and she had been the one who had told Hope all about Malala Yousafzai being shot for trying to go to school and get an education. Mum had been the person in the family that Hope felt closest to. The person she could talk to. But now she was gone.

Hope pulled her duvet over her head and tried to calm down. Then she rolled over and sniffed her pillow, letting the faint smell of Coco Mademoiselle soothe her to sleep.

CHAPTER 3

Hope stared at the new class seating plan. Her heart sank into her shoes when she saw who she'd be sitting beside. *Rebecca? Seriously?*

'Uh oh, shocker for you,' Katie said, looking over her shoulder.

Jayne patted her arm. 'It's only for a few weeks, you'll be OK.'

That was easy for Jayne to say. She'd got Hannah in the reshuffle and she was nice.

'Who did I get?' Katie scanned the list. 'Oh no! Not Laura.'

Jayne giggled. Laura had this really annoying habit of

22

twirling her hair around her fingers and then chewing it.

'I'm going to feel sick all day looking at her eating her hair. It's gross,' Katie said. 'Does she not get hairballs like cats do, and have to cough them up?'

They all giggled at the thought of Laura coughing up a lump of her hair.

Rebecca walked into the class and pushed her way past them to see the list. She flicked her long black hair back over her shoulder, hitting Hope in the eye.

'You have *got* to be kidding me,' she huffed, seeing Hope's name. Turning to her bestie, Mina, she rolled her eyes. 'Hope Dillon is *such* a loser.'

'She's right here,' Katie snapped, 'and *you're* the loser!'

Rebecca looked Katie up and down. 'Who even are you? You're like a nothing. Go back to your gang of nerds.'

Hope pulled Katie back before she could reply. There was no point fighting with Rebecca. It would just make things worse, and she was the one who had to sit next to her.

Mrs Lannigan arrived then, and everyone scurried to their new seats. Rebecca moved her chair as far away from Hope as possible, but when she realised she'd forgotten her history book, she had to share Hope's and move her chair right back in.

Rebecca's hair smelt of fresh flowers and was super shiny. She had a really pretty white hairband with tiny daisies on it. Hope reached up and felt her own hair. It was cut into a short bob.

When her mum died, Hope had cut all her hair off. She hadn't meant to do it: she had just gone into the bathroom the day after the funeral, pulled a pair of scissors out of the drawer and started cutting and cutting. Something about her hair falling all over the bathroom floor had made her feel better. But then Daisy had come in and screamed and grabbed the scissors from her hand. Her sister's screaming had snapped Hope out of the daze she was in. When she looked in the mirror, it was awful. Her hair was a mess. Poppy and Daisy had tried to even it out with the scissors, but eventually Dad had taken her to a hairdresser who had cut it really short and made it into a 'cute pixie cut'. There was nothing cute about it; she'd looked like a boy. It had taken ages to grow just below her ears. She was hoping that by the time she turned twelve, it would be back to shoulder length and she'd be able to put it in a ponytail again.

Rebecca twirled her rose-gold pen around her fingers. Everything she had was really cool. Her backpack was covered in rose-gold sequins, her pencil case was in the shape of red lips, her pens were all beautiful colours. She had diamond stud earrings and a necklace with a little diamond R on it. She even had a rose-gold Fitbit and matching iPhone 14. Her mum totally spoilt her rotten. Katie said that she'd heard her parents talking about Rebecca's parents' divorce and her mum had said that Janice had got a really scary lawyer who'd made Rebecca's rich dad give her a million euro in the divorce.

A million euro! Hope couldn't believe it. Rebecca was an actual millionaire. But Jayne pointed out that it was all very well to be rich, but Rebecca's dad had basically abandoned her. He now lived in England with his new wife, who was pregnant, and he hardly ever saw his daughter.

Hope did feel a bit bad when she heard that, but then Hope *never* saw her mum because she was actually dead. And they weren't rich either: Mum had worked as a nurse and, without her salary, money was super tight. Dad was always worried about paying the bills.

Hope imagined what she'd buy if she could have anything she wanted. It wouldn't be diamond stud earrings or an iPhone: she'd just buy hair extensions to try to get her hair back to how it was when her mum was alive.

The day dragged on and Hope tried to ignore Rebecca as much as possible. But it wasn't easy. Rebecca sighed and pouted and put lip gloss on whenever Mrs Lannigan had her back turned. Hope tried to focus on what Mrs Lannigan was saying; she wanted to do well in school, but she found it harder to concentrate since Mum's death. Mum always used to tell her that she was smart and that if she focused and tried her best then she could be anything she wanted to be. Hope wanted to become a doctor and find the cure for cancer. She wanted to make sure that no one else's mum died of ovarian cancer. She wanted to make sure no other kid had to suffer the heartbreaking loss she'd suffered.

Rebecca smacked her lips together for the millionth time. Her lip gloss smelt of strawberry. Initially, Hope had liked it, but now that she had been sitting beside Rebecca for six hours, the smell of her lip gloss and all of her smelly pens was making her feel sick. Hope turned her face away and bent over her maths book.

'Who cares about stupid long division?' Rebecca moaned. 'How's it going to help me in my modelling career?'

Hope rolled her eyes. Rebecca was always going on about how she was going to be a model and live in New York one day. Hope had to admit that Rebecca was pretty, but so were lots of girls.

'Even models need to work out how to pay their rent and bills,' Hope pointed out.

'I'll just get my mum's accountant to do all that,' said Rebecca, flicking back her hair.

'Well, I don't have an accountant, so can you please stop talking so I can listen?'

Rebecca leant in closer. 'Oh, I know you don't have an accountant. Your family is too poor to afford one. I know your dad is only dating my mum for her money. He's just a gold-digger, but he won't get a penny. Mum isn't even into him, she's just bored.'

Hope felt her blood boil. How dare Rebecca accuse her lovely dad of being a gold-digger? She spun around and shoved Rebecca in the arm.

Rebecca fell off her chair and landed on her bum. 'Oh my God, Hope assaulted me!' she shrieked. 'Mrs Lannigan, Hope physically attacked me.'

The teacher came rushing over. 'What happened here?'

'Hope didn't do anything,' Katie said. 'Rebecca was swinging back on her chair and it fell over.'

'I was not!' Rebecca's face was bright red.

'Yes, she was,' Jayne piped up. 'I saw it too. She was doing what you always tell us not to, Mrs Lannigan, swinging back on two legs of the chair, and *bam*, she fell.'

'Up you get,' Mrs Lannigan said, glaring at Rebecca. 'I

have told you a million times not to swing on the chairs. Now, sit up and not another word out of you.'

Rebecca stood up. Her face was now a deep shade of purple. 'HOPE PUSHED ME. SHE NEEDS TO BE PUNISHED!' she roared.

Mrs Lannigan's eyes narrowed. 'I think you need to calm down, Rebecca, and remember who you are talking to. Go and sit at the back of the class, and do not speak again until you are ready to apologise to me,' she said in an ice-cold voice.

Rebecca stormed to the back of the classroom and noisily sat down, muttering under her breath.

Hope hadn't meant for Rebecca to actually fall off her chair, but it was pretty funny. She grinned over at her friends. She felt all warm inside. She was lucky: she had the two best friends in the world. But she also knew that she was going to have to stop her dad going out with Janice. Whatever it took, she needed to break them up.

CHAPTER 4

ope sat in the kitchen in front of the laptop and felt her heart sink. The world was being destroyed by greenhouse gas emissions. The website said that a good way to reduce global warming was to reduce your own carbon footprint.

Hope googled how to do that. She found out that not driving petrol or diesel cars helped. Stopping eating meat and dairy, or at least cutting back on them. Turning the heating in your house down a notch or, even better, off. Using less water, showering more quickly, not leaving the water running when you brushed your teeth. Cutting down on single-use plastic and making sure to recycle. Not flying anywhere ... The list was long, very long. Hope's head hurt.

How could she help Greta save the world when there was so much to do? She took a deep breath and remembered Mum saying, 'When you feel overwhelmed, just take things one step at a time.' Hope decided she was going to start with small steps.

At dinner that night, when everyone was sitting down at the table, Hope made an announcement. 'OK, so we need to make some changes to help save the planet.'

'Here we go.' Poppy rolled her eyes.

Hope ignored her. 'We have to start eating less meat and dairy, using less water, walking to school and cycling everywhere, and never ever get on a plane again.'

'What are you on about?' Daisy asked, as she shovelled a large piece of hamburger into her mouth. 'I love meat and milk and cheese. I'm not giving them up – are we supposed to starve because of your latest obsession? How long is this one going to last?'

'Shush and let Hope finish,' Dad said. 'Go on, love.'

'Cows and sheep produce one-third of all methane emissions.'

'Could you please try to speak in English?' Poppy asked.

Hope tried to remember exactly what she'd read. 'Methane is one of the main greenhouse gases. If we don't do something about them, we're all going to die.' Hope hadn't meant to get emotional, she had planned to be calm and cool, but it was scary. Greta had said that the Earth was dying.

Poppy slapped down her fork. 'Drama queen! Dad, can you please talk to her? I am not giving up milk and I'm not going to cycle or walk everywhere just because Hope's got some ridiculous new obsession.'

'Hold on now, girls, your sister is right,' Dad said, smiling encouragingly at Hope. 'We *should* be doing more to help with the whole climate-change issue.'

Daisy smirked at him. 'OK, Dad, so you're going to walk to work from now on, are you?'

'Well, obviously I can't do that – my work is too far.'

'You *could* cycle,' Hope noted. 'It's only ten kilometres. I worked it out, and it would only take you about thirty minutes. You're always saying you want to get fitter but don't have the time. This could be your way of getting exercise into your day.'

'Yeah, Dad.' Daisy giggled. 'You should definitely cycle.'

He cleared his throat. 'Well now, Hope, I couldn't cycle in the rain and arrive to work soaking wet, could I? I'll look into it in the summertime, maybe.'

Hope had all the answers prepared. 'You can buy really good wet-weather gear that will keep you totally dry. You can order it online. Think of all the money you'd save on petrol.'

'If Dad's cycling to work in the lashing rain, does that mean that we'd have to walk to school?' Poppy asked.

'Yes,' said Hope. 'Why not? School is only three point two kilometres away. I calculated it last night.'

'I'm sure you did,' Poppy hissed, 'but I am not walking three point two kilometres with my massive bag of books on my back in the pelting rain.'

'To be fair now, Hope, Poppy has a point,' Dad said. 'Your schoolbags are very heavy, and I think it's best if I continue to drop you off on my way to work. I'll try to use the car less at the weekends, though – how about that?'

Hope felt deflated. *Still*, she thought, *Greta hadn't given up when she was sitting alone outside the Swedish government building and everyone was laughing at her. She'd kept going.*

'Well, if you won't give up the car, then we need to stop eating meat and dairy.'

'Why?' Daisy demanded. 'What possible harm can eating cheese do?'

Hope repeated what she'd read online: 'Cows and sheep burp and fart out methane all the time. One cow can produce up to two hundred kilograms of methane a year.'

Daisy and Poppy looked at each other and fell about laughing. 'Cow farts!' They laughed and laughed as Hope got crosser and crosser.

'Brrrrrp – oops, climate-change alert!' Daisy screeched, laughing.

'Brrrrp – oh no, I farted toxic gas,' Poppy snorted, cracking up.

Even Dad was laughing. Hope felt her blood boil.

'This is *not* funny. This is serious,' she said, raising her voice over their laughter.

'If I eat meat and I burp, am *I* destroying the planet too?' Poppy asked.

'Dad's farts are super smelly! I bet he's burning a hole in the ozone layer all by himself,' Daisy hooted.

Hope felt her eyes sting with tears. She shoved her chair back and stood up. 'If Mum was here, *she'd* listen to me. She'd take me seriously. She'd be on my side. You're all horrible and stupid. I hate you!'

She ran to her bedroom and hid under her duvet, sobbing.

Ten minutes later, there was a gentle knock on the door.

'Go away,' Hope said through tears.

The door opened and she heard a tray being placed on her bedside locker. 'We're sorry, pet,' Dad said. 'We were being silly. I think it's wonderful that you care so much about the planet, and we're all going to help you. Isn't that right, girls?'

'Yes, Dad. Sorry, Hope,' the twins drawled, not sounding one bit sorry.

Hope felt Dad's hand on her back through the duvet. 'Your mum would be very proud of you,' he said softly.

Hope waited for them all to leave the room and pulled the duvet down. She looked at the tray beside her bed. On it was a tub of her favourite Ben and Jerry's Cookie Dough ice cream and a glass of milk – two dairy products. She sighed. She had a long way to go to teach her family about helping the environment.

Hope was starving and she did love Ben and Jerry's ice cream, but she just couldn't allow herself to eat it. She had to be strong like Greta. She went downstairs, put the ice cream back in the freezer and ate a banana instead.

Being a climate-change role model was not going to be easy.

Chapter 5

Hope tried not to freak out as she heard the water cascading down in the shower, next to her bedroom. She watched her clock tick ... Then she jumped out of bed, ran out of her bedroom and thumped on the bathroom door.

'Get out!' she shouted.

No response.

'Turn off the shower.'

Still nothing.

'You've been in there for fifteen minutes!' Hope roared. 'That's nearly a hundred and twenty litres of water you've wasted.'

She heard the shower switch off. Finally. She turned to go back to her bedroom as her heart began to slow down. The bathroom door was flung open and she felt a hand grab her shoulder and spin her around.

'What the hell?' Poppy asked, her face bright red with anger. She was standing wrapped in a towel, soaking wet. Drips of water streamed down her body onto the carpet. Her hair was covered in shampoo.

'Every minute you spend in the shower uses up almost eight litres of water.'

'What are you talking about?'

'Wasting water,' Hope explained.

'Oh my God, I thought something really bad had happened. Did you seriously just get me out of the shower to bang on about wasting water?'

'You've been in there for fifteen minutes.'

'So what?'

'So what? So you're wasting water – and energy we need to preserve.'

'I don't care about wasting water or cow farts or walking to school. Get out of my face or I swear I will kill you!' her sister roared at her. 'I've got shampoo in my eyes now because of you.'

Hope was well used to her sisters shouting at her. She really didn't care. As long as she got them to stop wasting water, she was happy. 'If you'd stayed in for five more minutes you would have wasted—'

'Oh my God, will you ever just shut up?!' Poppy cut across her and stormed back into the bathroom, slamming the door.

Hope went back into her bedroom and sat on her bed. She looked at the picture of Greta Thunberg that she'd pinned to her wall and sighed. It was going to be tough trying to change her family's bad habits, but she had to try.

Greta had been fifteen when she started spending her school days outside the Swedish parliament, holding a sign asking for action on climate change. Hope was only eleven, but you were never too young to start working for change. Whatever her sisters said, she wasn't going to give up. She didn't want to let Greta down and she knew Mum would be cheering her on.

Dad stood at the bottom of the stairs shouting up. 'Come on, girls, I told you I had an early meeting today. Chop chop.'

Poppy came down holding a tissue over her left eye.

'What's wrong with your eye?' Dad asked.

'Your stupid younger daughter forced me out of the shower because I was using too much water and the world was about to collapse and I got shampoo in my eye and it stings.'

Hope saw Dad hide a smile. 'Well now, you do spend far too long in the shower in the mornings and it *is* a waste of water.'

Poppy glared at her father. 'Do *not* start with me about wasting water. I am not in the mood. I may actually be blind because of Hope.'

Dad patted her on the shoulder. 'I think you'll survive.'

Daisy came out of the kitchen, waving her phone in the air. 'Who switched off the charger?'

'I did,' said Hope. 'It's really bad to leave things plugged in all night.' She started to pull on her coat.

Daisy shoved her phone in front of Hope's face. 'Really? Is it? Well, it's also incredibly annoying when you wake up to find your phone is dead. What the hell am I supposed to do without my phone?'

'You're not supposed to have them during school hours,' Dad reminded her.

'Oh, for goodness' sake, Dad, everyone has them in

38

school. I swear, Hope, if you ever do that again, I will kill you before Poppy does.'

Dad jangled his keys. 'Enough of the violent talk. Hope is just trying to help the planet. Now, let's go.'

Hope pulled her school-coat hood up. 'I'm walking, Dad.'

'It's lashing rain, Hope, please get into the car.'

'Saving the planet begins with small steps,' Hope said, putting her gloves on.

Dad bent down to eye level with his daughter. 'Hope, I am driving your sisters anyway. You aren't saving emissions by not getting into the car. It's raining and I don't want you to get sick. If you really want to, you can walk to school on dry days.'

Hope shook her head. 'No, Dad, if everyone in this family is determined not to do anything to help the planet, then I'll just have to work extra hard. Greta's parents weren't happy with her campaigning in the beginning, either. But she kept going.'

Dad ran his hands through his hair in exasperation. 'Hope, I can't let you walk to school and sit in soaking wet shoes all day. It's bad parenting.'

Hope looked directly into her father's eyes. 'I'm an

activist now, Dad – I'm saving the planet. Nothing you do or say can stop me.'

Dad paused. 'Well, sweetheart, I am still the parent here and I'm *telling* you to get into the car.'

Hope shook her head stubbornly.

'Oh, just leave her,' Poppy said. 'She'll get sick and that'll teach her a lesson.'

'Hope,' Dad said softly, 'please get into the car. I promised your mum that I would look after you and I'm doing my best. I will support you not eating meat or dairy, and help you drag your sisters out of the shower, and I will allow you to walk to school on dry days, but for now, today, I need you to get into the car.'

Hope thought about it and then gave in. If getting a lift to school from Dad today meant that he promised to commit to helping her, she'd compromise. She silently got into the car, ignoring her sisters' filthy looks and sarcastic comments.

They could say whatever they wanted; she knew that she was doing the right thing. She just needed to figure out how to persuade other people to join her.

Jayne took a large bite of her cheese sandwich. 'Let me get this straight. We need to give up all cheese, milk, butter, yoghurt and ice cream?'

Hope nodded.

'But that means that I can't eat any of my lunch,' Jayne pointed out. 'I've got a cheese sandwich, a yoghurt and a carton of milk.'

'I know, but you can have tomato and onion or hummus sandwiches instead.'

'I hate mushy tomato sandwiches and hummus looks like vomit,' Jayne pointed out.

'I actually quite like it,' Katie said, 'although my dad says it's food for chickens, not humans – *chick*-peas.' She grinned.

'I'll die of starvation if I have to give up dairy.' Jayne shoved the rest of her cheese sandwich into her mouth, as if she was afraid that Hope might ask her to dump it.

Hope sighed. It wasn't easy trying to get people to save the world. 'OK, how about you give up *one* dairy product, then?'

Jayne looked down at her lunch. 'I guess I could give up yoghurts. I like them, but I could live without them.'

41

'How can anyone give up milk? What would you put on your cereal?' Katie asked.

Hope hadn't actually thought about that. 'I dunno, like, soya milk or almond milk or something, I guess.'

Katie made vomit noises. 'Have you ever tasted them? My mum drinks almond milk and it's the most disgusting thing ever. I could never put that on my Rice Krispies.'

'I've tried soya milk and it actually tastes fine,' Jayne said. 'Mum is trying to get us to switch to it. Maybe I'll try it on my cereal tomorrow.'

'My mum eats coconut milk yoghurts – I tried them and they're not too bad, so I guess I could try eating more of them,' Katie said.

'But I can't give up cheese. I love cheese,' Jayne said.

'OK, it's a start.' Hope rubbed her eyes. She'd have to do more research into alternative cheese options. If she was going to try to get people to give up meat and dairy, she needed to test out and suggest good alternatives.

In class later that day, as Rebecca twirled her hair and, in the seat in front, Laura *ate* her hair, Hope made lists in her head of what she needed Dad to get in the supermarket on Saturday. No more steak or burgers. Lots of vegetables and fruit and nuts. Hope only really liked peas and carrots, so she was going to find this tough. Could she still put crisps on the shopping list? Hope loved her cheese and onion crisps, but were they bad? They came in plastic bags – that couldn't be good for the environment.

Maybe she should go vegan, like Greta, Hope thought. But would that mean she had to eat loads of beans and pulses? She didn't really like beans either, especially red kidney beans, yuck. Mum used to say that if you ate something ten times you'd eventually like it. But it hadn't worked with broccoli, or red kidney beans, or tuna.

Hope's head throbbed. She'd have to google what vegans ate when she got home. Beside her, Rebecca's phone vibrated. They weren't allowed phones in the classroom, you had to leave them in the lockers, but Rebecca always had hers with her, hidden in her skirt pocket.

Hope watched from the corner of her eye as Rebecca snuck her phone out and read the text message. Hope knew it was wrong to read other people's private messages, but she couldn't help herself.

Sorry, Becs, have to cancel you coming over this weekend. Olga is finding the pregnancy difficult and needs me to look after her.

Hope saw Rebecca's face fall. She watched her type back.

Thanks a lot Dad. I haven't seen you in ten weeks!!! Olga always comes first.

Rebecca threw her phone into her bag and let her long hair fall over her face like a curtain. Nobody else but Hope, sitting so close to Rebecca, could see the teardrops falling onto her school skirt. Hope felt sorry for her. Even if she *was* a huge pain, she was obviously missing her dad and Hope knew what it was like to miss a parent.

She fished a tissue out of her bag – since Mum had died Hope always had tissues in her bag, because she never knew when she'd feel like crying. She handed one to Rebecca.

'What are you doing?' Rebecca snapped.

'I thought you might need this,' Hope whispered.

Rebecca, with her hair still covering her face, handed the tissue back. 'Why? I'm fine.' She wiped her eyes with her hands. Then, flicking her hair off her face, she turned to Hope, her eyes full of rage.

'Did you read my text message?'

'No,' Hope lied. 'But I saw you were sad.'

'Well, I'm not. I just have a cold. Stop staring at me, you freak.'

Rebecca put her hand up and asked to go to the toilet. She pushed past Hope as she left the classroom. The pity Hope had felt for her classmate disappeared as quickly as it had come.

CHAPTER 6

Hope stood outside the twins' bedroom. Her dad had told her to ask the twins what they wanted in the weekly grocery shop. She craned her neck and peeped in at her sisters through the half-open door. Poppy was lounging on her bed while Daisy was at her desk, examining her face with a magnifying mirror.

'Why are my lips so small?' Daisy groaned. 'You're so lucky, Poppy, you got Mum's lips. Hope and I got Dad's skinny little ones.'

It was true, Poppy looked like Mum – full lips, shiny black hair and amazing green eyes. Daisy and Hope looked like Dad, boring brown hair, blue eyes – not amazing sea-blue eyes, just normal ones – and thin lips.

'Yeah, but you got the long skinny legs and I got short stumpy ones,' Poppy said.

'Yeah, but you got actual boobs and I got nothing – I barely have two fried eggs. I still don't need a bra and I'm fifteen!' Daisy groaned.

'As Mum always said, we're both gorgeous in our own unique ways,' Poppy reminded her twin.

'Yeah, I remember her saying she was glad we weren't identical because it meant we were able to be our own person.'

Hope remembered Mum saying that all the time. She said it was harder for identical twins because people assumed they had the same personalities and likes and dislikes. But if you didn't look like your twin, people treated you as an individual, not a pair. Hope agreed with Mum: both of her sisters were really pretty in different ways.

Hope looked like Dad, which wasn't a bad thing because Dad was quite handsome, but she had one thing of her mum's that she loved – her dimple. When Hope smiled, she had a deep dimple in her right cheek, and Mum had had the exact same one. Sometimes they'd smile at each other just to see their dimples and laugh. Hope missed Mum's laugh; it was her favourite sound.

Dad said that Hope also had Mum's caring personality. He said that Mum felt empathy for people and things and that Hope had inherited that special trait. He didn't say the twins had, but he did say they'd inherited her sense of fun.

'What are you doing? Spying on us?' Daisy spotted Hope lurking at their door.

'No, I'm doing the shopping list for Dad. What do you want on it?'

'Did you put tampons on it? Dad always forgets.'

'I think he gets embarrassed. Maybe you should buy those yourself in the pharmacy,' Hope suggested.

'No way. He needs to realise that having daughters means buying sanitary products.'

Hope wrote 'tampons' on the list. 'Anything else?' she asked.

'Do you have ice cream and a jar of Nutella?' Poppy asked.

Hope had neither on her list. She was trying to do a vegan-focused, environmentally friendly shopping list.

Poppy narrowed her eyes. 'Show me that list.'

'No, it's fine, I'll put those things on it,' Hope lied.

But Poppy had jumped up and yanked the list out of her hand before she had time to react. Hope tried to grab it back, but Daisy pushed her onto her bed and sat on top of her.

Poppy's eyes widened as she read.

'What is it? What's on it?' Daisy asked.

'Soya milk, pumpkin seeds, almonds, lentils, brown rice, dried mango, coconut ice cream, millions of vegetables and fruit and ... oh my God, are you serious? Tofu?' Poppy's mouth dropped open in shock.

'What? Is this a joke?' Daisy asked Hope. 'Are you seriously going to ask Dad to buy this crap? What exactly are we supposed to eat?'

Hope kept her voice steady. 'We need to eat more consciously, so I thought we could do vegetable bakes with tofu, and fruit salads with coconut ice cream – it's supposed to be nice.'

Poppy waved the list in her younger sister's face. 'Says who? Says some Swedish nerd who probably never tasted Ben and Jerry's ice cream in her life. She probably eats snow for dessert and thinks it's a treat.'

Daisy grabbed the list and wrote down all the things the twins wanted. She handed it back to Hope. '*Now* you can give it to Dad. If *you* want to eat tofu and pumpkin seeds, knock yourself out, but you are not ruining our lives with your latest obsession.'

Hope felt anger rising up through her chest and into her throat. 'All you ever think about is yourselves. The world is dying, our planet is crumbling – can't you see we need to do something?'

Poppy pushed her out of the room and closed the door. 'Go and preach to your dorky friends, and you can all have a midnight feast of dried mango and brown rice!' she shouted. Hope heard the twins roaring laughing as she stormed downstairs.

Dad was sitting in the kitchen with the radio on, reading the Saturday newspaper. He was humming along to some ancient song. It was nice to see him looking relaxed. His foot tapped along to the music as he sipped his coffee and read his paper.

Sensing he was being watched, he looked up. 'Hey, what's up?'

'I have the shopping list.'

'Ah thanks, love, what would I do without you?' Dad held out his hand and Hope passed him the list.

He glanced at it. 'Looks like a healthy list. I know you're keen for us to stay away from dairy, but I will be getting some cow's milk and a little cheese.' Before Hope could respond, Dad added, 'But I will also get some soya milk and vegan cheese and give it a try. Deal?'

Hope nodded. 'Deal.'

She popped a bagel in the toaster. She looked at the plastic wrapper. Everything in the cupboard was wrapped in some form of plastic. Even the cereals were in plastic bags inside their cardboard boxes. Hope stared at all the food – pasta, rice, crackers, crisps, biscuits, cereal bars … everything was packaged in plastic. She felt her heart racing. How was she going to deal with all this plastic?

'Dad?'

'Mmmm?' he said, not looking up from his newspaper.

'We need to start using less plastic and recycling more.'

'We do recycle, love. We have our green bin.'

'I know, but today in the supermarket, I'm going to make sure we buy as few plastic-wrapped goods as possible, and then we can unwrap the plastic wrapping we don't need at the checkout. I read online that the supermarkets have to take the plastic back if you do that.'

Dad put his newspaper down. 'Hang on a minute now, Hope, I'm not sure about unwrapping stuff at the checkout. You know how long the queues are on Saturday mornings and, besides, we can't have food falling out all over the place.'

Hope patted her father on the shoulder. 'Don't worry, Dad, I'll do it all.'

Her dad sighed, but said nothing.

Dad wasn't thrilled when Hope said they had to cycle to the supermarket. It was on the edge of town, about eight kilometres away. By the time they got there, he was sweating and his face was bright red. They locked their bikes and then spent almost two hours in the supermarket going through the aisles, trying to find the least-packaged goods to buy. Hope could feel Dad losing patience, but he didn't snap at her, and when they finally got to the checkout he smiled and kissed her on the forehead.

'You're a good girl, Hope. I know you're doing your best to help the environment, and I'm proud of you and I know your mum would be too.'

Hope smiled up at him and then started removing the items from their packages. She took the plastic off the peppers, the bananas, the cheese ...

'What are you doing?' the checkout lady asked. Her badge said her name was Linda.

'I'm taking off the unnecessary plastic wrapping from the food. Bananas have their own natural wrapper – their skin. They don't need plastic.'

'What am I supposed to do with this, then?' Linda asked, holding up a lump of plastic.

'You have to show your manager and tell him that he needs to tell his suppliers that they have to stop using so much plastic.'

'Look, love, I have four kids and I've been up since five a.m. I'm tired and I really don't want to have to deal with a load of plastic all over my checkout.'

'But we have to save our planet.'

'You're slowing down the line. People are going to start complaining,' Linda said.

'Sorry, we'll hurry along.' Dad leant over Hope and started ramming food into the shopping bags they'd bought with them.

But then Hope took the wrapping off the pack of twelve toilet rolls. The rolls wobbled, then fell and bounced all over the supermarket floor. Dad said a very bad word under his breath.

Linda stood up. 'That's it, love, you can save the planet somewhere else. You're holding up the queue with all this nonsense. Go home and play video games like a normal kid and stop annoying people.'

'Now hang on a minute,' said Dad, standing up, holding three toilet rolls under his arm. 'My daughter is trying to help the environment. You should be encouraging her, not trying to shame her. I think it's wonderful that she's trying to do something useful rather than sitting on a couch staring at a screen.'

'Go and save the world down the road in Lidl, then, and let us get our shopping done!' a man queueing behind them shouted.

'Don't you—' Dad began to shout back, but Hope put a hand on his arm. She was afraid a fight was going to break out.

'It's OK, Dad. Let's just go.'

They scooped up the remaining toilet rolls and hurried out of the shop. While they'd been inside it had begun to rain ... heavily.

Dad muttered, 'I told you we should have driven,' under his breath as he tried to put the heavier bags on his back carrier and hang the others from his handlebars. He gave the lighter bags to Hope to put in her bicycle basket.

They set off in the lashing rain to cycle the eight kilometres home. Within minutes, they were soaked. Dad was cycling in front and, as they reached the halfway point, one of the bags on the back of his bike fell off and a big box of washing powder exploded all over the road.

Dad pulled his bike over to the fence on the side of the road and tried to steady it, but the bike kept falling over because the bags hanging from it were so heavy. Hope parked her bike beside his and ran over to help.

They tried to scoop some of the powder back into the box, but it had turned lumpy in the rain and the biodegradable box was now a soggy mess.

They were about to give up when they heard a loud *beeeeeeeeeeep*. They jumped, and looked up to see Janice and Rebecca parking beside them in their brand-new Range Rover. Janice rolled down the window.

'Oh my goodness, I *thought* it was you. What's going on, Joe? You're soaked through.'

Dad smiled. 'It's a long story.'

'Can I give you a lift home?'

'That would be great.'

'But we can cycle ...' said Hope.

Dad glared at her. 'We are not going to make it home in this rain. Get into the car, Hope.'

'Muuuum, the seats are going to get wet,' Rebecca moaned.

'Shush, don't be rude,' Janice said to her daughter.

Neither she nor Rebecca got out of the car to help Hope and her dad load up the heavy shopping bags. The boot opened automatically, so Janice never even had to leave her seat. They put the bags in the boot, leaving the soggy washing powder box beside their locked bikes. Dad said he'd come back and pick the bikes up later.

While Rebecca sat up front with her mother, Dad and Hope sat in the back, dripping wet. Hope was worried about their wet clothes ruining the beautiful cream seats. The car was so clean and new and fancy. She sat on her hands to try to protect the leather.

'Joe, I don't think you've met my daughter, Rebecca.'

'Hi Rebecca, I think I've seen you at a few school events,' Dad said in a super-friendly voice.

Ignoring him, Rebecca didn't look up from her phone.

'I recognise you too, Hope. How are you?' Janice tried to cover up for her daughter's rudeness.

'I'm fine, thank you,' Hope said politely.

An awkward silence fell on the car.

'So, about tonight,' Janice said. 'You know because I cancelled our date last night that Rebecca isn't going to London to stay with her dad this weekend after all – because he's too busy, apparently. So I was thinking, why don't you come to my house and I'll cook dinner? In fact,' Janice said, looking at Hope and her dad in the rear-view mirror, 'why don't you bring all three girls? They can hang out together and have fun.'

'What?!' Hope and Rebecca said at the same time.

'No way, Mum.' Rebecca wasn't staring at her phone anymore – she was glaring at her mother.

'Rebecca!' Janice frowned at her.

'I think you should go out together, on your own,' Hope suggested.

'Yeah, me too,' Rebecca agreed, throwing a glance Hope's way.

'I can't leave you in the house on your own,' Janice reminded her daughter.

'I'll be fine, stop fussing.'

'You're eleven, you are not staying in the house on your own. I'm sorry, but it's not my fault your dad's so selfish.'

'He's not selfish, he's just—'

'Too busy with his new wife to see his own daughter,' Janice snapped.

Rebecca's face fell. Hope felt a bit sorry for her. It must hurt to have your dad cancel on you all the time.

'I think it's a lovely idea, and we'd all be delighted to come – thanks, Janice,' Dad said, trying to smooth things over.

'Super.' Janice pulled up outside their house. 'See you about seven.'

Rebecca glared at her mother, who ignored her.

Hope walked up the path to their house carrying the bags of groceries with a heavy heart. Dinner with Rebecca? Seriously? Could this day get any worse?

CHAPTER 7

The twins shook their heads. 'No way. There is *no way* we are going to dinner in some randomer's house,' said Daisy.

Dad frowned. 'Yes, you are going and that's the end of it. Janice has invited us all to dinner with her and Rebecca and we are going to go and be polite.'

'Take Hope, she's in Rebecca's class. Leave us at home,' said Poppy.

'She invited all of us.' Dad's voice was beginning to rise.

'So tell her we're sick,' Daisy suggested.

'Yeah, tell her we have the flu or that we have something

59

really infectious and gross like leprosy and we can't leave the house,' Poppy added.

Dad thumped his soggy hand down on the kitchen table. 'We are going and that is the end of it. Now, I'm going to take off my wet clothes and have a long hot shower.'

'Not too long, Dad,' Hope said.

Dad sighed. 'Fine, a quick shower.'

He left the kitchen and Poppy turned on Hope. 'This is all your fault.'

'How is it *my* fault that Janice invited us over?'

'Because you made Dad cycle to the supermarket in the lashing rain and Janice had to give you a lift home. If you had let Dad drive, like a normal person, none of this would have happened. Now he's all grumpy and wet and forcing us to go to this awful dinner.'

'It's not my fault. Rebecca's father dumped her, and Janice can't leave her on her own, so if you want to blame someone, blame him.' Hope stomped out of the kitchen and went up to her room to dry off.

She was furious. Furious with the rain, furious with the washing powder box smashing on the road, furious with stupid Janice and even stupider Rebecca. How was she going to get through a whole evening with the one girl in her class she really couldn't stand?

Hope spent ages choosing what to wear. She didn't want to look like she'd made an effort, but she also didn't want to look like a dork. Eventually, she went for black skinny jeans, her lilac sweatshirt and white trainers.

When she came downstairs, Dad was waiting. He was wearing his good jeans and a smart shirt. He looked very handsome; no wonder Janice liked him. Hope had always felt proud when she was out with her mum and dad. They were a 'gorgeous couple inside and out', as her gran always said. Both of them had 'big, generous hearts'.

Hope didn't know what Dad saw in Janice. She was so different to Mum. Janice had shoulder-length bleached blonde hair and big brown eyes that she wore loads of black eyeliner around, which made her look a bit like a panda bear. She also wore short skirts and very tight tops, like she was about to go out clubbing at any minute. Mum had always looked really elegant, but Janice looked ... well ... like she was trying to be a teenager again.

'You look lovely, Hope – now, where are your sisters?' Dad called up the stairs to the twins.

'Keep your hair on, we're ready,' Daisy said, as she and Poppy walked down the stairs.

Dad glanced up. 'No,' he said. 'Absolutely not. You are not going to dinner dressed like that. Put some clothes on.'

'Hello! These *are* clothes,' Daisy said.

The twins were wearing cut-off denim shorts and crop tops.

'They are small pieces of material that barely cover your bodies,' Dad pointed out. 'Up you go and put on something that covers at least seventy per cent of your skin.'

'This is called fashion, Dad. It's something you have no clue about,' Poppy said.

Dad shook his finger at her. 'Poppy, I know one thing, and that is that you are not going out dressed like that. So go back up and put on some actual clothes.'

'Oh my God, you are so old and clueless,' Daisy huffed.

'You are fifteen and I'm your father. Now get dressed. Besides, it's three degrees outside – you'll freeze.'

'We're fifteen and a half, and we *are* dressed. And we don't feel the cold like old people.' Poppy stomped back up the stairs, followed by Daisy.

Dad sighed and rubbed his eyes. He looked at Hope. 'When you become a teenager, please don't constantly push the boundaries and argue with me incessantly. It's exhausting. Stay as lovely as you are now, *please*.'

Hope smiled. 'I'll try.'

Dad pulled her into his arms for a hug. 'I know you will. You have your mum's personality. The twins are more like your Aunt Louise, lively and mischievous. I'll have to keep my eye on them ...'

Hope snuggled into his warm body and felt safe and loved.

They waited and waited for the twins. Eventually, Hope went up to see what was going on. The girls' bedroom was a complete mess. There were clothes everywhere and both twins were in their bras and knickers.

'Come on!' Hope said. 'Dad's about to lose it, we're already late.'

'We can't find anything to wear to this stupid dinner,' Poppy complained.

Hope pointed at the piles of clothes on the ground. 'Just wear jeans and a top, like me.'

Poppy laughed. 'We're not dressing like little kids.'

'We could wear our cream cargoes and our Nike sports crop tops, with our denim jackets over?' Daisy suggested.

'Yeah, that could look good. I'll wear the black top, you can wear the red one,' Poppy said.

They got dressed. Dad was not going to be happy with their stomachs showing, but at least their legs were covered and, if they kept the jackets on, so were their arms.

Daisy pulled her crop top over her head. 'What's she like, anyway?' she asked Hope.

'Who? Rebecca?'

'Duh, no. Who cares about the stupid kid? I mean Janice. What's Janice like?'

Hope shrugged. 'I dunno; she seems OK. I don't know her.'

'Dad seems to like her,' Poppy said as she buttoned up her cargoes.

'God, do you think she could end up being our new stepmother?' Daisy's eyes widened.

'Eww, no way. Dad's just lonely,' Poppy said.

'Yeah, but lonely people get married,' Daisy pointed out.

'NO!' Hope shouted. 'Dad is not marrying anyone. No way. No no no.'

64

'Calm down,' Daisy hissed at her.

'If he does,' Poppy said, applying lip gloss, 'you'll have a stepsister the same age as you, so you'll be like twins too.'

Hope felt tears prick her eyes. Her fists scrunched together. 'There is *no way* that Rebecca is ever becoming my stepsister. Never ever ever.' The thought of it made her stomach turn.

'Chill out, we're just winding you up. Dad's not going to marry anyone,' Poppy said.

But how do you know? Hope thought. *How can you be sure?* Daisy was right: lonely people *did* get married. Dad was lonely. He might make a bad decision just because he wanted company.

Hope decided she needed to spend more time with him. She'd make sure he was never lonely. She'd stay up late and watch his favourite football team, Liverpool, play matches. Mum had supported Liverpool too. Their wedding song had been the Liverpool anthem, 'You'll Never Walk Alone'. Hope found football really boring, but she would do whatever it took to keep Dad company. There was no way and no how that Rebecca was going to become her stepsister and Janice her stepmum.

CHAPTER 8

Hope had only seen Rebecca's house from the road, and you couldn't really see much because it was hidden behind big trees.

The electric gates opened, and they drove up the long curving driveway.

'Oh my God, it's a mansion!' Daisy said.

'They must be minted,' Poppy added.

'It's not about the size of someone's house, it's about who they are as a person,' Dad reminded them. 'But I have to say, it *is* a beautiful house.'

It was an amazing house. Hope stared up at the big windows and the balcony that curved out above the front door. Every window had a box filled with flowers outside it. Pink roses climbed up the sides of the walls. Two big trees, one either side of the huge front door, were wrapped in twinkly lights. It was stunning.

The front door opened and Janice stood framed in the light of the hall.

'Are you kidding me?' Daisy exclaimed.

'*She's* wearing denim shorts.' Poppy glared at her father.

Janice was wearing denim shorts, high-heeled ankle boots and a bright-blue silk blouse.

'So, Dad, what do you think of your girlfriend's outfit?' Daisy asked.

'She's not my girlfriend and she looks ... well ... she looks ... um, nice.'

'So, you don't have a problem with Janice showing too much skin?' Poppy poked her father in the arm.

'Well ... I, um ... she's ... it's a very youthful look, but ... Oh come on, get out of the car, we're late as it is.'

Janice waved at them as they walked to the door. 'Welcome.' She leant up and kissed Dad on the cheek. Her shiny lip gloss was now on his face. Hope's stomach twisted into a knot. She wanted to rub it off.

Dad introduced the twins, who quickly shook Janice's hand and then rushed past her into the house. Hope, Dad and Janice followed behind. The hall was enormous. Two big staircases, covered in a rich red carpet, swept up both sides of the hall to a balcony. The hall had a cream marble tile floor and there was a big round table in the middle with a huge blue vase filled with white flowers. Hanging from the middle of the high ceiling was a light made out of hundreds of wires covered in tiny crystals, all lit up. It was magical.

'You have a lovely home,' Dad said to Janice.

'It's the one good thing my rotten ex-husband left me,' Janice said, winking at Dad. Hope shuddered.

Hope caught up with the twins and followed them into the living room, where Rebecca was sitting on the couch watching TV.

'Rebecca, say hello to our guests. Joe and I are going to grab some wine in the kitchen,' Janice called out as she led Dad away. Rebecca slowly stood up and turned towards them. She was wearing a white sweatshirt with 'Balmain' written across the front, and a black ruffled tulle miniskirt with 'Balmain' written along the waistband, paired with white trainers with 'Gucci' printed on the side.

'Well, we don't need to ask her where she got her outfit! Could those labels *be* any bigger?' Daisy muttered.

'I love her Gucci trainers, but they're crazy expensive,' Poppy whispered back.

Hope felt all wrong. Her jeans were from Penneys and her sweatshirt was a hand-me-down from the twins. She had been happy with her outfit, but now, seeing Rebecca looking incredible in all her designer clothes, she suddenly felt really self-conscious. Hope pulled the sleeves of her sweatshirt down over her hands and said nothing.

'Hi, nice trainers.' Poppy broke the silence.

Rebecca flicked her hair. 'Yeah, my dad got them for me in America. You can't get them here or even online yet. They're next season.'

'Yes, well her dad does spoil her. Only child and all that,' Janice said, as she and Dad entered the room holding glasses full of red wine. 'Although with his new baby on the way that's bound to change.'

Hope watched Rebecca's eyes flash.

Janice didn't seem to notice. 'Right, well, dinner won't be ready for another twenty minutes, so why don't you show the girls your bedroom, Rebecca?'

'My bedroom?' Rebecca glared at her mother. 'Why would I want to bring a bunch of strangers up there?'

'Hope's not a stranger and you've just had it painted and re-carpeted. It looks lovely; show the girls.'

'Right, let's go.' Daisy gave Rebecca a little nudge. 'Show us your new carpet.'

Hope was so glad her sisters were with her. It was awkward enough anyway, but if she'd been on her own it would have been so much worse.

'So, what's for dinner? I'm starving,' Poppy said, looking at Rebecca as they walked up the stairs.

'Thai chicken curry.'

'Yum.' Poppy was pleased.

'My mum's a crap cook, so she got the food made. She's pretending she cooked it to impress your dad. I don't know why.'

'Because she obviously fancies him,' Daisy said.

Rebecca snorted. 'I don't think so.'

'She looks pretty keen to me in her teeny-tiny shorts.' Poppy grinned.

Rebecca's face went red. 'She's so embarrassing – I told her to wear something normal. Since Dad left she's started wearing all these clothes that are way too young for her.'

Their feet sank into the plush carpet in the corridor as

they made their way to Rebecca's bedroom. Rebecca opened up a double door and they entered her room. But it wasn't a bedroom, it was a luxury suite, like in a really posh hotel.

Hope gasped. The new carpet was a light grey colour and so soft, it was like walking on pillows. The walls were painted a beautiful grey-blue tone. In the centre of the room was Rebecca's bed. A big double four-poster with white tulle draped all down the sides and fairy lights wrapped around the posts, twinkling brightly. In one corner of the room was a big desk with shelves down both sides. The shelves were filled with candles and jewellery boxes. Hope spotted photos of Rebecca with her dad and her mum and a few with her annoying friend Mina.

On the other side of the bed was a big egg chair with a fluffy baby-blue cushion on it. It was Hope's dream to have an egg chair. They were so cool. But she certainly wasn't going to admit that to Rebecca.

'Where do keep your clothes?' Daisy asked.

'Here.' Rebecca opened a door that led to a big walk-in wardrobe. There were rows and rows of clothes, all hung by colour. The wall at the back had shelves filled with shoes, mostly trainers, in every colour and style. In the middle of the wardrobe was a big vanity unit. It was covered with make-up.

Poppy picked up a MAC eyeshadow palette. 'Why do you have all this make-up? You're, like, ten.'

'I'm almost twelve, actually, and I like make-up.'

Daisy was staring at the racks of clothes with her mouth open. 'You are so lucky. This is amazing. This wardrobe is bigger than our entire bedroom.'

Hope winced. She didn't want Daisy telling Rebecca that she was better than them. Yes, her bedroom was amazing, but so what? She was still a cow.

'Do you have an en-suite?' Daisy asked.

'Of course.' Rebecca led them over to the other side of the bedroom and opened another door, which revealed a big marble bathroom. It had steps up to a big round jacuzzi bath. On the left was a huge shower and on the right was a big sink with a mirror surrounded by light bulbs, like in the movies.

Hope tried not to show how impressed she was. She didn't want Rebecca to see how much Hope wished she had all of this. Her bedroom at home was the old boxroom. It was too small to fit a double bed. It had one single bed and a small wardrobe. Hope did her homework at the kitchen table. There was no desk or separate bathroom – or egg chair.

Daisy whooped. 'Wow, I would never get out of the bath if I lived here.'

'I hate baths. They take too long, it's boring,' Rebecca said.

Poppy made a rude sign behind her back, which made Hope giggle.

They went back into the bedroom. Rebecca sat on her bed, Daisy sat in the egg chair and Poppy sat in the desk chair. Hope didn't know what to do, so she just stood beside Poppy, leaning against the desk.

'So, what's the story with your dad?' Poppy broke the silence.

'What do you mean?' Rebecca glared at her.

'Where does he live and what's all this about him having another kid?'

'He lives in London now. He has to, because of tax bills and all that. His new wife, Olga, is from Russia, but they met in London. They have an amazing house there. London is so cool, so much better than this dump. I'm moving there as soon as I finish school.'

'And they're having a baby?' Poppy asked.

'Yeah, my baby sister is due soon.'

'Lucky girl, she can get all your hand-me-down designer clothes,' Daisy said.

Rebecca wrinkled her nose. 'There is no way Olga would let her child wear anything second-hand. She's going to be a totally spoilt princess.'

Daisy looked at Hope and winked.

'You should sell your old clothes on eBay – you could make some serious cash,' Poppy suggested.

'I'm not selling my clothes, thank you very much. Mum gives them to the homeless or to our cleaning lady.'

Poppy cracked up. 'A homeless person does *not* need a Balmain tulle skirt, they need coats, blankets and food.'

Daisy, swinging in the egg chair, laughed loudly.

'Whatever. I'm bored with this conversation,' Rebecca huffed.

'Fine then, what do you want to talk about?' Daisy asked. Rebecca's bedroom's wow-factor was wearing off and it looked like Daisy was getting annoyed with her rudeness.

Rebecca twirled her hair. 'I dunno.' She pulled her phone out and began to scroll.

'OK, so I guess this stimulating conversation is over,'

Poppy said loudly. 'Why don't we check out Rebecca's make-up?' She grinned at Daisy.

Rebecca's head snapped up. 'What? No. Don't touch my stuff.'

'You're going to have to learn to share with a new sister coming along. We'll help you practise.' Poppy gave Rebecca a big fake smile.

'I swear, if you touch my make-up, I'll—'

'DINNER!' Janice shouted up the stairs.

Phew, Hope thought. Dinner had just stopped a fight. Mind you, she would have liked to see Rebecca try to fight the twins. She would have had no chance. None. Zero.

CHAPTER 9

ope pushed her chicken around her plate and ate
the rice and green beans. She didn't like green
beans, they felt all squishy and squelchy in her
mouth, but if she was going to try to be a vegan like Greta,
she had to get to like vegetables or she'd die of hunger.

Daisy reached over and spiked one of Hope's chicken
pieces with her fork.

'Do you not like it?' Janice asked.

'Oh no, it's lovely, thank you.'

'Hope's gone veggie – or is it vegan?' Daisy asked Hope,
who blushed.

'Oh, your dad should have told me …' Janice looked
at Dad.

'I didn't really know. Hope has been making a lot of changes lately based on saving the planet. I'm not sure *what* she's eating at the moment.'

'Vegans are so boring,' said Rebecca. 'Mina tried it once and stopped after five hours. She couldn't live without ice cream.'

'Well now, I think it's a good thing to be passionate about something, and Hope's passion is the environment these days.'

Hope felt good that Dad was defending her.

'My passion is chilli Doritos,' Poppy said, grinning.

'Mine's Oreo milkshakes.' Daisy snorted. 'What's yours, Rebecca? Sharing your things with others?' The twins cracked up laughing.

'I agree with you, Joe,' Janice piped up. 'We all need to make changes. I don't use throw-away coffee cups anymore, I have my own keep cup. I'm doing my bit.'

'Did you know that sixteen billion coffee cups are used every year worldwide and 99.75 per cent of them are not recycled?' Hope suddenly said.

'My goodness, no I didn't. That is a lot of cups.' Janice was genuinely shocked.

'Are you sure it isn't 99.74 per cent?' Daisy said.

'I heard 99.76 per cent,' Poppy added.

'Stop it, you two,' Dad warned. 'It's great that Hope is interested in helping save the environment. You two could do with a bit more awareness.'

'You too, Rebecca,' Janice added.

Rebecca's eyes narrowed. 'I have no intention of going around like some complete loser droning on about recycling coffee cups and eating grass. I'm actually embarrassed for you, Hope. You sound like such a nerd.'

Poppy put her knife and fork down on her plate and leant forward. 'Do not speak to my sister like that. Hope is brilliant. She's a bit out-there, but she's great and we won't have anyone slagging her off, least of all you.'

Daisy waved a fork in Rebecca's direction. 'Hope does go on a bit about the planet and all that, but she's our sister and no one is allowed to be mean about her, ever. Get it?'

Hope beamed up at her two sisters.

'OK, I think we all need to calm down,' Dad said, jumping in to try to stop a full-on fight.

'Why don't we have dessert?' Janice said quickly. She carried over a big plate of meringues filled with cream and strawberries and served them each a bowlful.

'Wow, this looks fantastic, Janice, thank you,' Dad said.

'It's not like she actually made it,' Rebecca snarled.

'Who cares? It's delicious,' Poppy said, her mouth already full.

Hope really wanted to eat it, but meringues were made with eggs, and cream was not allowed either if you were vegan. Hope really wanted to be good and try to commit to veganism like Greta, but she also really wanted to try one of the amazing meringues. *No*, she thought, straightening up. *I have to make sacrifices to save the world.* Hope tried to block out the 'Mmmmmm' sounds that her sisters were making as they scoffed down the delicious dessert.

Chapter 10

Hope took a deep breath and stuck the list up on the bathroom door. She knew there would be a reaction to it, but she had to do something about all the water they were using as a family. She had to stop the waste.

She placed the egg timer beside the shower and went back into her bedroom to get dressed for school. She was pulling her school jumper over her head when she heard a loud yell.

'You have *got* to be joking! Daaaaaaaad, Hope has finally lost it.'

Hope peeped out from her bedroom and saw Daisy pointing at the list on the bathroom door.

'Hope, can you come out here, please, love?' Dad called.

Hope stepped out of her bedroom just as Poppy came out of the twins' room to see what was going on.

'What's happening?' Poppy asked.

'This,' Daisy said, pointing at the list. 'Hope now wants us to count our toilet flushes. She says we need to cut down because apparently last week she counted us flushing a hundred and sixteen times.'

'Which is equal to eight hundred and twelve litres of water,' Hope interjected. 'And that's not including the washing machine and the dishwasher and showers and all of that.'

'So what exactly are you suggesting here?' Dad asked.

'That we don't flush all the time,' Hope said.

'So you're saying that we leave our poos floating about because you want to save water?' Daisy shook her head.

'No, you can flush poos, but if it's just a small wee, leave it and the next person can flush when they go to the toilet. You know the saying, "if it's yellow, let it mellow; if it's brown, flush it down".'

'Urgh!' Daisy grimaced. 'Dad, please do something.' She glared at her father.

'Hope, I think that might be stretching things a bit far. I'm fine with cutting back on shower time and not running the tap when we brush our teeth, but I'm afraid I'm not with you on the toilet flushing,' said Dad.

'What's that?' Poppy spotted the red egg timer.

'It's to time our showers. Five minutes is the maximum time we should be taking,' Hope explained.

'How am I supposed to shampoo and condition my hair and rinse it out in five minutes? Do you want us all going around with greasy hair and smelly bodies and a loo full of wee? What is *wrong* with you?' Poppy picked up the egg timer and shook it in Hope's face.

'I'm trying to save the planet!' Hope shouted. 'You are so selfish, all of you. You don't care about anyone but yourselves. We have to *do* something, before it's too late.'

Dad put his hand on her shoulder. 'Hey now, don't upset yourself. We'll work out a shorter shower time, but you mustn't get yourself so worked up, Hope.'

Hope shook her head. They just didn't get it. If everyone in the world continued living the same selfish way, then the planet would be destroyed. She'd been reading up about it and watching loads of videos. People had to listen to Greta, and David Attenborough, and all the other climate-change activists. Global warming could only be slowed down if *everyone* made an effort.

'If you'll all excuse me, I'd like to have my three-second shower now,' Daisy said, slamming the bathroom door shut behind her.

Hope went downstairs to make herself a hummus sandwich and walk to school. How could she make people see how important saving the environment was?

When she got to school, Jayne and Katie were waiting for her, dying to hear all about the dinner at Rebecca's. She filled them in.

'Wow, her bedroom sounds incredible,' Jayne said.

'What was the name of the designer on her clothes?' Katie asked.

'Balmain,' Hope said. 'The twins say it's super posh.'

'I've never heard of Balmain,' Katie said, googling it on her phone. 'Oh my God, is this the skirt?' She showed Hope a picture.

Hope nodded.

'It's four hundred and ninety euro,' Katie gasped.

'What a waste of money,' Jayne said. She spent most of

her spare time in her brother's old Manchester United football shirts. Fashion was not her thing, and she could not understand why anyone would spend lots of money on clothes.

'It's gorgeous, though ... did it look super cute on?' Katie gazed at the photo.

Hope had to admit that it had. 'Yeah.'

'Was all the stuff in her walk-in wardrobe designer too?' Katie asked.

'Pretty much.'

'Lucky her.'

'I don't think she's lucky at all. She's a spoilt cow whose dad basically ignores her, she's miserable about it and she deals with it by being mean to everyone, especially Hope,' Jayne said.

'I know, but I'd still love to have her clothes,' Katie said. She looked up and quickly put her phone in her pocket as Rebecca swished by, Mina at her side.

'Poor you,' Mina was saying. '*And* you had the twin sisters to deal with too.' Mina looked horrified.

'Yeah, it was a total drag. They were, like, so obsessed with all my stuff. It was kind of embarrassing. They've obviously never seen designer clothes before.'

Hope felt her face flush. How dare Rebecca be so rude about the twins?

'Just ignore her,' Katie whispered. 'She wants to upset you, don't let her.'

'I had so much fun with my dad this weekend,' Jayne said loudly. 'He took me to a football match and then we went for chicken wings. He is such a great dad. He never lets me down and always wants to spend time with me.'

Jayne winked at Hope as they watched Rebecca's face redden.

Hope sighed. She didn't like Rebecca, but she could see how much it hurt her that her dad ignored her. And as someone who missed her mum every day, Hope knew the pain of an absent parent, although *her* parent was never coming back. Still, it must be hard for Rebecca, and it would probably get even harder when the new baby arrived. Although she knew Jayne was only trying to defend her, she felt uncomfortable about rubbing Rebecca's face in it.

Rebecca was bright red now. 'I can't wait to leave this dump of a school and go to my private senior school. There are so many freaks and geeks here, I can't wait to get away,' she hissed.

Before anyone could say anything else, Mrs Lannigan

walked in. Hope sat down beside Rebecca, but Rebecca turned her back on her and leant as far away as was possible without falling off her chair.

'Take one and pass them around, please,' said their teacher. She handed out a pile of printed-out pages. 'Today we're going to talk about plastic and what it's doing to our oceans. These printouts are full of information I have pulled together from different climate-change groups, explaining the dangers of plastic pollution. We all need to be more aware of the damage that plastic causes.'

Hope sat up. *Finally*, something interesting to listen to instead of rock formation and photosynthesis.

'You must be happy,' Rebecca hissed. 'This boring crap is just what you nerds like to bore everyone about.'

Hope ignored Rebecca and, instead of listening to Mrs Lannigan, who was taking far too long to get to the interesting bits, she read ahead. She knew that the oceans were being polluted by plastic – everyone did. Well, maybe not Daisy and Poppy. They never listened in class and did badly in exams, but they didn't care because they had decided they were going to go on *Love Island* and be famous for being the 'fun Irish twins' and make loads of money from endorsements. They hadn't told Dad their plan yet, but Hope had heard them discussing it.

Unlike her sisters, Hope *did* want to do well in school. Mum had always said Hope was the smartest of them all. She'd tried so hard to get the twins to work harder in school, but they just didn't care.

Hope didn't think she was super smart, but she did have a good memory and she liked learning. Not boring subjects like maths, but history and geography and science; she loved those three the most. She had been reading up about climate change, but she still had so much to learn. She knew that she needed to be more like Greta and be able to inform people about the dangers the world was facing with all the facts and figures about the environment at her fingertips. When Greta talked, adults listened, because she knew her subject super well and she had researched and read loads of books and watched documentaries and talked to experts and become best friends with David Attenborough. Hope knew that she needed to be better informed.

Turning over the class handout, Hope read on: 'Every year eight million tonnes of plastic ends up in our oceans. Over seven hundred different species of marine animals have eaten or got caught up in plastic. But the good news is that by understanding the issue and taking action, you can help change the future and make our oceans cleaner and safer.'

Hope exhaled with relief. People *could* turn back the clock and make the oceans safe again for all the fish and the other creatures that lived in it. They just needed to make more effort. Like she was trying to.

'Half of the plastic we produce is designed to be used once (single-use plastic) and is then thrown away: water bottles, straws, food wrappers ... All of this plastic takes over 400 years to break down and decompose. Animals and birds are getting trapped and tangled up and even strangled by the plastic waste. We have to do something before it's too late.'

Hope was shocked. She knew things were bad, but this was really awful. The poor fish and birds! She had to try harder to get her family to stop using single-use plastic. They could all drink from reusable water bottles, reuse their shopping bags and not buy things wrapped in plastic. The only problem was, after the last shopping fiasco, with the rain and the checkout lady shouting at her and the washing powder spilling all over the road, Hope wasn't sure that Dad would ever let her go shopping with him again. Still, she'd have to try. Maybe if she let him drive to the shops and took the extra plastic wrapping off the shopping *before* they got to the checkout, it would cause fewer problems.

When Mrs Lannigan finally got to the end of the page, Hope raised her hand. She was shaking and nervous, but

Greta did things that made her scared all the time, all activists did, so Hope had to be brave.

'Yes, Hope?' Mrs Lannigan said.

'I was just thinking that maybe we could all do something to help clean up the oceans. It says lots of plastic gets blown into the drains and the sea from parks and over-stuffed park bins, so maybe we could organise a park clean-up?'

'Will you ever shut your stupid mouth?' hissed Rebecca beside her. 'Over my dead body am I cleaning up other people's manky trash!'

'I think that's a wonderful idea,' Mrs Lannigan said enthusiastically, drowning out Rebecca's whiny voice. She beamed at Hope. 'Good girl. I'll leave you to organise the class into five separate groups, and I'll talk to the headmistress about a date for a class outing to clean up our town park.'

Rebecca's hand shot up. 'Sorry, Mrs Lannigan, but I think it's extremely dangerous for us to be picking up trash. Who knows what we might find? Disgusting things like needles full of drugs or cans of beer or plastic dog poo bags. We could get a disease or something.'

Mina spoke up in support of her friend. 'Yeah. And I know my parents wouldn't want me to spend school time working as a bin man.'

Mrs Lannigan raised her hand to silence them. 'Nobody is going to catch a disease, Rebecca, and no one is working as a bin man, Mina. We will simply be picking up litter as volunteers, and we will have gloves and litter-picker sticks. Your lives will not be at risk. No one ever became ill or died from picking up litter in their local park.'

Hope grinned. *Go Mrs Lannigan.*

The teacher clapped her hands. 'I want to hear no more nonsense about this excellent idea. Hope Dillon is in charge of sorting out the groups and I will co-ordinate with her to organise gloves, bags and litter-picker sticks for everyone.'

'I'm happy to help,' said Katie. 'I think it's a great idea.'

'Yeah, me too, and we'll get off school for it,' Jayne spoke up.

'Happy to pick up junk in the cold and rain? You're all pathetic.' Rebecca pouted. 'I can promise you that I'll be out sick that day.'

Good, Hope thought. *We don't need your nasty attitude or comments.* Hope was wishing she could tell her exciting news about setting up a class project to the one person she couldn't talk to: Mum. Mum would have been so proud of her. She would have hugged her and made her a hot chocolate to celebrate and then helped her to organise it. Hope fought back tears. 'Focus on the positives, sweetheart,' Mum would always say. Hope was going to try really hard to do that. This was a good first step to saving the planet: everything started with small steps.

CHAPTER 11

ope gazed at Greta on the screen and let her words sink in. Greta had been so angry giving that speech, furious and passionate and holding back tears. She was talking to serious politicians and world leaders at the actual United Nations and she was giving out to them and telling them that they had stolen her dreams. She shouted that people were dying and ecosystems were collapsing, but all people cared about was money and economic growth. She even shouted, 'How dare you?' at them.

Hope gasped. Had Greta actually said, 'How dare you?' to a room full of world leaders? Greta was way braver than Hope was. She couldn't even stand up to her own sisters. She was pathetic.

There was Greta, who had been bullied in school, often hiding in the school toilets to escape her bullies, now doing everything she could to save the planet.

There was Greta, who was autistic and was afraid of lots of things, being so brave and speaking in front of hundreds of people, telling them they had to take action.

There was Greta, who had horrible messages posted on her social media accounts by nasty trolls, still going out and fighting for what she believed in.

Mum always told the twins that people who posted nasty comments were sad, unhappy people with nothing going on in their lives. Last year, Poppy had got a nasty comment about a photo she'd put up on her Instagram, of her in a miniskirt. The person had written, 'Nobody with your fat legs should wear short skirts. Cover up your thunder thighs.' The account had a fake name, so Poppy hadn't even known who it was. She had been crying and staring at her thighs, asking, 'Are they fat? Should I only wear maxiskirts?'

Daisy had been in tears too. The twins were so close they were like two halves of one person. Once, when Poppy fell out of a tree in the garden and broke her arm, Daisy – who had been in her bedroom when it happened – said she felt a sharp pain in her arm the exact second it happened.

Anyway, Daisy had wanted to attack the nasty person by posting a mean reply to their nasty message, but Mum had said, 'Don't ever respond to nasty comments.' She said that if you replied you were just going to start a huge fight.

'These people *want* you to react. They want to know they have hurt you. Knowing they have made you feel bad gives them a little power buzz. So, ignoring them is the best thing you can do.'

Daisy had listened and nodded, but the minute Mum's back was turned, she'd posted a rude message back. Daisy called the person a '[very rude word] loser and a [very rude word] freak' and she said if they ever posted anything about her sister again, she would go the police and track them down.

Hope had thought Daisy was a bit silly saying she'd go to the police about some random person on Instagram saying her sister's legs were fat. She reckoned the police were probably too busy catching serious criminals and putting bad guys in prison to worry about things like that. Though obviously Hope hadn't said that to Daisy.

Greta didn't have a twin sister to defend her, but nothing stopped her trying to get her message out into the world. Nothing stopped her trying to persuade other people to make changes to save the planet. Hope knew she had to do more. But what?

Hope checked her vegetable burgers and called everyone in for dinner. She'd decided that the only way to persuade Dad and her sisters to become vegetarian was to cook them nice vegetarian dinners. This was her first attempt and she was really pleased with the result. It had taken ages. Way longer than she'd thought it would. She was tired but happy.

Dad came in first. 'That smells and looks delicious, pet, well done you.'

Daisy and Poppy followed.

'Burgers! Hope, you star. I'm starving.' Poppy threw herself into her chair, picked up the burger bun and took a big bite.

Hope waited, holding her breath.

Poppy chewed and chewed. Her face scrunched up, her eyes narrowed, her nose twitched and then she let out a roar. 'What the hell is this?'

Daisy, who had only just taken a bite, looked worried. 'What?' she asked with her mouth full, bits of burger bun flying out of her mouth and onto the table.

Poppy glared at Hope. 'This is not a burger.'

'Yes, it is,' Hope replied.

Beside her, Dad was sniffing his burger. 'It doesn't look like meat,' he mumbled.

'That's because it isn't meat,' Poppy raged. 'It's just disgusting mush.'

Daisy, having just chewed through the bun and got to the burger part, began to make gagging noises. She rushed over to the bin and spat her mouthful of food into it.

'Daisy!' Dad snapped. 'Stop that. Hope has made a big effort to cook us all dinner and we should be grateful.'

'Grateful for being poisoned.' Daisy drank deeply from a glass of water.

'Why should we be grateful for being tricked into thinking we were getting burgers?' Poppy demanded to know.

'What is in the burger, Hope?' Dad asked, ignoring the other two.

Hope chewed her burger and pretended to love it. She didn't love it, but it wasn't bad. It was OK and she was determined to give up meat, so she would learn to love it.

'The main ingredient is sweet potato and then onions and sweetcorn, and chilli and herbs too.'

'It's actually really nice, love.' Dad took a large bite and chewed. 'Very tasty. We are all very grateful to you for cooking us dinner.'

'I'm not,' Poppy said.

'Me neither,' Daisy said.

Hope closed her eyes and channelled Greta. She slammed her hand down on the table and stood up. 'How dare you?!' she shouted. 'People are dying, animals are becoming extinct, oceans are being destroyed by pollution, and all you can do is moan.'

Hope felt her heart pounding in her chest. She felt strong, brave and passionate. She was going to help Greta. She was going to help the planet. She could do this, she could change people's minds. She would make her family see what needed to be done, one step at a time.

'OK, so Hope has officially lost it,' Poppy said, making twirling movements with her finger beside her head.

'Off-the-charts crazy,' Daisy agreed.

Dad stood up and gently helped Hope to sit back down. 'Hope, love, sit down for a minute like a good girl and have a drink of water.' He patted her on the shoulder.

'There is no need to get yourself into a state, it's not good for you.'

Hope shrugged him off. 'If we don't fight this, we will ruin our world. We can't just sit around doing nothing, Dad. We have to act.'

'Well, Hope,' Poppy said, hands on her hips, 'while you're busy making shouty speeches, your family is starving to death. If you try to force us to eat this muck, *we* are the ones who will become extinct.'

CHAPTER 12

ope looked out of the classroom window, watching the rain lashing down, and hoped that the weather would be better this time next week when they were doing their clean-up of the local park. She wanted the other girls to enjoy the activity so that they'd do it again, or just pick up trash if they saw it on the street. If every single person regularly picked up one piece of rubbish on the street, that would make a huge difference, she was sure.

Beside her, Rebecca twirled her silver charm bracelet around her wrist. Hope couldn't help looking at it. The charms were gorgeous. There were six of them – an ice cream, a flip-flop, a lipstick, a heart, a star and a sparkly letter R.

'Are you excited about going to London?' Mina whispered from across the aisle.

'Obviously.' Rebecca flicked her hair back. 'I'm going to spend all weekend shopping. Dad always gives me loads of money to treat myself to new clothes.'

Mina sighed. 'You are so lucky. I wish my dad was like yours.'

What? Did Mina honestly want a dad who cheated on her mum and then went to live in a different country with his new wife and had a new baby on the way that he was going to see every day, when he only saw Rebecca every now and then? Hope didn't think so.

Hope's dad might have no spare money to spoil her with, but he was a great dad. He was always there for her and was really kind and nice to her and the twins, even when they drove him crazy.

'Yeah,' Rebecca agreed, 'my dad is really cool, so much better than my boring mum. All she does is nag me. I can't wait to get away from her. As soon as I can, I'm moving to London to live with my dad full time. I'm going to ask him this weekend.'

'Won't your mum miss you, though?' Mina asked.

Rebecca shrugged. 'She'll be fine. She has a boyfriend.'

Hope froze. If Rebecca moved to London, then Janice would have no one and she'd cling to Dad. What if Dad *did* marry her and then she moved in? Even if Rebecca went to live in London, she'd still come home to visit. And if Janice was living with them, then Rebecca would have to as well! No way. Hope couldn't handle having her as a stepsister. That just *couldn't* happen.

When she got home, Hope went into the TV room, where the twins were lying at opposite ends of the couch watching their favourite show, *Ginny & Georgia*.

'No,' Daisy said, as soon as she saw Hope.

'What?' Hope was confused.

'Whatever you are going to tell us, we don't want to hear it. We're sick of your save the Earth speeches.'

Poppy grinned and turned up the volume on the TV.

'It's about Dad marrying Janice.' Hope had to shout to be heard over the noise.

Both of her sisters' heads turned to look at her. *Ha, I have their attention now.*

Poppy paused the TV. 'What?' she asked.

'Dad's marrying Janice?' Daisy looked horrified.

101

'No. Well, not yet. But Rebecca wants to move to London to live with her dad, which means that Janice will be on her own and she'll be really lonely and she'll probably try to force Dad to marry her and then she'll move in and be our stepmother,' Hope blurted out.

'There is no way Rebecca's dad will let her live with him. He's about to have a new baby and his young wife won't want that nasty eleven-year-old annoying her,' Daisy said.

Poppy sat up and tucked her legs under her. 'And, if Dad *does* ever marry Janice, we're moving into Janice's house. If we're going to have an annoying stepmother, at least let's get something out of it.'

'I'm getting Rebecca's room,' Daisy said.

'Well, then I'm getting the egg chair,' Poppy said.

Hope couldn't believe it. Why were her sisters not taking this seriously? Dad couldn't marry Janice. Not ever. Mum was his wife. This was Mum's house, they were Mum's daughters and no one, no woman, was ever going to replace her.

'We have to break them up,' Hope said.

'He's having her over to dinner tonight. Why don't you cook her one of your disgusting vegan dinners? That'll scare her off!' Daisy giggled.

'Or you could give her one of your boring speeches about climate change,' Poppy said, grinning, before the twins cracked up laughing.

Hope didn't feel it coming, but suddenly a huge wave of emotion hit her. She hadn't meant to cry, but she found herself sobbing and she couldn't stop. She bent over and cried and cried.

Poppy and Daisy jumped up. 'Hey, we were only teasing ... come on, Hope, don't cry ... we're sorry ...'

'I miss Muuuuuuuuuuuuum,' Hope sobbed. 'I miss her so much.'

'So do we,' Poppy said, tears in her eyes.

'We miss her really badly, Hope.' Daisy sniffed.

'You never talk about her.'

'It hurts too much,' Daisy admitted.

'I get so angry when I think about Mum and why she had to die and why everyone else has a mum and we don't.' Poppy wiped tears from her cheeks.

'I don't want anyone replacing her,' Hope said. 'Mum was so special.'

Daisy put her arm around Hope's shoulder. 'No one is ever going to replace Mum, don't worry.'

'Ever.' Poppy squeezed Hope's hand.

Hope gave them both a watery smile. It was nice to see them upset. Not nice in a mean way, but nice to know that they missed Mum too. Sometimes Hope wondered if they ever thought about Mum because they never said anything. But she could see they did. She could see they were really sad too. She was glad she wasn't the only one who missed her.

Daisy blew her nose and then said, 'Right, it's Operation Get Rid of Janice tonight.'

'Janice is going down,' Poppy agreed.

Hope giggled. They were a team. For once it didn't feel like the twins and then Hope. For once it felt like the three Dillon sisters together, and it was brilliant.

CHAPTER 13

The three sisters sat in the twins' room, plotting and planning.

'We can't be mean or rude to her, or Dad will be annoyed with us,' Daisy warned them.

'We have to be nasty in a nice way,' Poppy agreed.

'How can you be nasty in a nice way?' Hope asked.

Daisy stood up and pretended to greet Janice. 'Janice, so good to see you again. It's so cool that you are still wearing such short skirts at your age.'

Hope giggled.

'So sad that your husband dumped you, why *was* that?' Poppy sniggered.

Hope gasped. 'You can't say that, it's too mean.'

Poppy put her hands on her hips. 'Do you want to get rid of her or not?'

Hope nodded.

'Well then, we have to scare her off. You have to toughen up, Hope,' Poppy told her.

Hope scrunched her fists together. She'd be strong. She'd even be mean if it meant getting rid of Janice.

Dad came home from work shortly after the sisters' conversation. He called the girls downstairs.

'I think I mentioned I'm having Janice over for dinner at eight. Is it OK if I order you pizza tonight? I want to keep the kitchen clear for cooking – and tidy it up a bit too.'

'Sure, Dad, no problem,' Daisy said.

'We'll help you tidy up,' Poppy added.

'Really?' Dad looked surprised.

The girls nodded, looking all innocent.

'That'd be great. I'm going to make beef stroganoff.' Dad turned to Hope. 'I know you'd rather I didn't buy red meat, but it's a special occasion.'

Why is it a special occasion? Hope's heart thundered in her chest. Was Dad going to ask Janice to marry him? Surely not – they'd only been going out for about two months. She looked at Daisy.

'What's so special about tonight, Dad?' Daisy asked, keeping her voice casual.

Dad looked down. 'It's just that it's the first time I've ever cooked for anyone apart from you lot and your mum.'

Silence.

No one knew what to say. Hope felt her heart slowing down. He wasn't going to propose to Janice, but he must like her if he was inviting her to dinner in the house and was cooking for her.

Poppy broke the silence. 'We'd better get on with it, then – we don't want to poison her, do we?'

Everyone fake-laughed and the tension in the room was broken.

Hope refused to chop the meat, but she helped cut up the mushrooms. She stood side by side with her dad, chopping, while the twins cleaned up the kitchen, noisily shoving everything into drawers and cupboards.

Daisy found the good tablecloth and the good plates and set the table for two. Poppy put two blue candlesticks in the middle of the table and inserted two white candles.

Hope was worried they were making it too romantic.

When the casserole dish was in the oven, Dad raced upstairs to get ready. The girls were finally alone.

'Right, here's what we're going to do. Leave the comments to me and Poppy,' Daisy said to Hope. 'You say nothing, but offer to help Dad serve the dinner. When he's not looking, drop these chilli seeds into Janice's dinner. I scraped every seed out of the two chillies in the fridge. They'll burn her mouth off.'

Daisy pointed to a teaspoon, hidden behind the kettle, that was covered in chilli seeds. She was a genius.

Poppy put her hands on Hope's shoulders. 'We're going to pretend we're into all your save the world stuff. So don't look too surprised. We've got the fake poo I got last year for April Fools' Day and we're putting it in the downstairs loo. We need you to put your 'Only flush once a year – save water' list thing up on the door of the loo when Dad's not looking. We have a couple of other ideas too. Whatever happens, act as if what we're doing is completely normal. Got it?'

Hope nodded. Her stomach was doing flips with nerves and excitement. It was fun to be in on an adventure with her big sisters.

Janice arrived at ten past eight. Before Dad had even got up from his chair, Poppy was already galloping out of the room to open the door, Daisy following fast behind.

Hope peeped out from the TV room.

'Hiiiiiiii, Janice. OMG, you look amazing,' Poppy said.

'Yeah, you really do,' Daisy agreed.

'Come in.' Dad ushered Janice inside.

'You are really rocking those skin-tight jeans. I'm not sure even *I'd* be brave enough to wear them,' Poppy said.

'I never imagined an older woman could actually wear them, but wow, here you are!' Daisy pretended to be impressed.

'Oh, well, I—'

Poppy cut across Janice: 'And your top is so sparkly, you look like you could be going to a nightclub.'

'Yeah, you really don't dress like an older person – you go for a much younger vibe,' Daisy said, smiling sweetly at Janice.

Hope covered her mouth to stop a giggle escaping.

Dad showed Janice into the kitchen, poured her a glass of wine and tried to close the door on the twins, but they followed him in. Hope snuck in behind them.

'Hi, Hope, how are you?' Janice asked. 'Are you finding Mrs Lannigan as awful as Rebecca does? She seems like a right old witch.'

Hope shook her head. 'No. Actually, I really like Mrs Lannigan. I think she's an excellent teacher and not a witch at all. My mum always said that some parents are far too quick to criticise teachers.'

Janice's cheeks went a bit red. 'Oh, well, I didn't mean ... I ... you know Rebecca exaggerates stories, so the teachers always sound worse than they really are.'

'My mum always knew when I was exaggerating. She could tell straight away,' said Hope.

Janice took a gulp of her wine.

'Right, girls, I think Janice and I would like some space now,' Dad said firmly.

'But you said we could help serve the dinner,' Poppy reminded him.

Dad brushed his hair out of his face and sighed. 'OK, but then you need to let us eat alone.'

Poppy got cold water from the fridge and filled up Janice's and Dad's water glasses and handed them each a napkin. While Dad was topping up Janice's wine, Daisy pushed a plate full of beef stroganoff towards Hope, who quickly mixed the chilli seeds into it. Daisy then carried the two plates over, being careful to put the spiked plate down in front of Janice.

'Thank you, this looks wonderful,' Janice said.

'Dad cooked it especially for you,' Poppy said.

'He spent ages making it. I'm sure you'll love it,' Daisy added, obviously hoping to increase the pressure on Janice.

'Bon appetit,' Poppy said, and they left the room.

When they were safely back in the TV room with the door closed, they all fell about laughing.

'Her mouth is going to be in flames!' Poppy giggled.

'And she's going to be too polite to say it's awful!' Daisy shrieked.

'What you said about her clothes was so bad,' Hope said. 'I never knew you could be nice and mean at the same time.'

'It's called being passive-aggressive,' Poppy explained to her little sister. 'It's like, you're insulting someone, but they don't realise it's an insult.'

'You guys are very good at it,' Hope said.

They smirked at her. 'We practise a lot at school.'

They heard the kitchen door open and someone

running to the bathroom. They opened the door a crack and peered out.

Janice was sprinting to the toilet. She pulled the door open and then they heard an 'Oh my God!'

'She's seen the poo,' Poppy whispered, and they all cracked up again. 'Shhhh, Dad's coming.'

Dad knocked gently on the toilet door. 'Janice, are you OK? Are you unwell?'

'I'm fine, I just need a minute,' Janice called out.

Dad went back into the kitchen. The girls could hear Janice freaking out in the toilet.

'Ooooooh, my mouth ... what did he put in it ... oh God, the pain ... it's like fire ... ooooooooh!'

A tiny part of Hope felt bad for making Janice eat so many chilli seeds, but then she thought about Rebecca becoming her stepsister and she stopped feeling bad.

Poppy walked over to the toilet door.

'What are you doing?' Daisy hissed.

Poppy winked at them and rattled the door handle loudly. 'Daisy, I know you're in there, probably doing a big stinky poo. Hurry up, I need to go and Hope's using the loo upstairs.'

Daisy covered her mouth to stop the snorting laughter from coming out.

No response from Janice. Poppy grinned at her sisters. 'DAISY, get out of there and you'd better flush your poo. I don't care what Hope says about wasting water, floating poos are disgusting.'

Hope and Daisy were now crying with laughter.

Dad came out of the kitchen to see what all the shouting was about.

'What are you doing?' he hissed, as Poppy rattled the door handle again. 'Janice is in there.'

Poppy pretended to be shocked. 'What? Oh no, I thought it was Daisy!' Poppy put her mouth close to the door and shouted, 'Sorry, Janice, I thought you were Daisy!'

She turned and walked towards the TV room, winking at Hope and Daisy, who were hiding behind the door, crying with laughter. They all huddled together and peeped out as Janice, red-faced and sweating, came out of the toilet.

'There seems to be a problem with your plumbing,' Janice muttered. 'The flush doesn't seem to be working. It was ... well, it was floating there when I went in. It wasn't me. I didn't do it ... I mean I didn't leave it ...' Janice tripped over her words.

'Oh God.' Dad covered his face with his hands. 'I'm mortified. Hope has this obsession with toilet flushing. She refuses to flush unless absolutely necessary. I'm so sorry. Please come back in and finish your dinner.'

'Actually, I'm not feeling very hungry.'

'Oh, did you not like the meal?' Dad looked crestfallen.

'No, it was nice, I just get full quickly, but I'd murder a glass of cold white wine.'

'Coming right up,' Dad said.

The three sisters high-fived each other. They had done a good job. Janice would never come back to the house again.

CHAPTER 14

The sisters waited for Janice to leave, but she didn't. She stayed on ... and on. At eleven, she was still in the kitchen, and when they stood outside the door, they could hear laughing.

'She's tougher than we thought,' Daisy noted. 'We practically poisoned her and then we really embarrassed her, but she's still here.'

'We'll have to think of something else,' Hope whispered.

'It's all gone very quiet,' Poppy said.

It was true: suddenly the laughing had stopped and there was silence.

'One of us has to go in,' Daisy said.

'It's your turn, Hope.'

'Why me?'

'Because you're the one who started this. Now go in there and see what's going on!' Daisy pulled the door handle down, opened the door a little and shoved Hope in.

She tripped over herself and landed on the floor of the kitchen. But as she fell, Hope saw them. Janice was sitting on Dad's knee and they were kissing. Actual kissing. Lips together, arms around each other.

Dad and Janice jumped up when they saw Hope collapsing through the door.

Dad went to pick Hope up. She shrugged him away. He had Janice's red lipstick on his lips. Hope wanted to get a towel and scrub it off. She felt rage rise up inside her.

'How could you?' she screamed at her father. 'How could you kiss someone else? What about Mum? You're acting as if she never existed. You're just moving on and forgetting her. I hate you.' Hope stormed out of the kitchen, then ran past the twins and up the stairs.

'Way to go, Hope,' she heard Daisy say as she ran past her.

But this wasn't an act. This wasn't a fake tantrum to get rid of Janice. This was real. Hope was angrier than she had ever been in her whole life.

She slammed her bedroom door shut, threw herself down on her bed and punched her pillow over and over again. She could hear muffled voices downstairs and then she heard the front door closing.

A minute later there was a gentle knock on her door. 'Hope, can I please come in?'

'Go away, Dad, I don't want to talk to you.'

The door opened and Dad came in. He gently sat on the edge of the bed. Hope turned her head away from him.

'I'm sorry, pet. I'm sorry if I upset you by being insensitive.'

'Yeah, you should be,' Daisy said, as she and Poppy came into the room.

'I shouldn't have invited Janice here to the house.'

'*Or* shoved your tongue down her throat,' Poppy added.

Dad coughed. 'I'm very sorry that you saw me ... uhm ... well ... having a cuddle with Janice.'

'Cuddle!' Daisy snorted. 'More like a big shift.'

Dad ignored the twins. 'I want you all to know that your mum was the love of my life. I miss her every single day. I will never ever forget her. She gave me the greatest gift of all – the three greatest gifts ever – my three girls. Me going out with Janice, or any other woman, is never going to take away what I had with your mum. She was my world, all of our worlds. But life does move on and if I'm being honest, I get a bit lonely sometimes. Going for dinner or to the cinema with Janice is just a bit of adult company for me. It's nothing else. No one will ever replace your mum.'

'But what if you fall in love with Janice?' Poppy's voice was quiet.

Dad paused. 'If I do, well then, I'll deal with that at the time, but for now she's just a friend.'

'A friend who you kiss,' Daisy reminded him.

Hope turned to face her dad. 'So you're never going to replace Mum and get married again?' she asked.

He looked down at his hands. 'I can't promise that, Hope. I don't know what the future holds – no one does. But I want you to know that I loved your mum with all my heart and nothing can change that. If I ever did fall in love again it would be different. And what will never ever change is how much I love the three of you. No matter who comes into our lives, you three will always be my priority. You are the most important people in my life and always will be.'

'What if you married a woman who had a son who was amazing at football and played striker for Manchester

United? Would we still be your number one then?' Poppy asked, raising an eyebrow.

Dad laughed. 'Come here, you lot, give your old dad a hug.'

They all sat on the bed and had a group hug. Daisy pulled away first. 'OK, enough of the soppy stuff.'

Dad kissed Hope on the forehead and left the room, the twins following. Hope felt better, but not totally reassured.

After all, Dad hadn't *actually* said he would never marry Janice.

CHAPTER 15

Hope woke up early and ran to the window. She threw back the curtains. Phew, it wasn't raining. It was a bit grey and a bit overcast, but there was no rain.

She washed herself with a facecloth in the bathroom sink. It used very little water and she was still clean. She washed under her arms, her neck, her face and her tummy.

She'd tried to get the twins to do the same a few days a week instead of showers every day, but they had absolutely point-blank refused.

'I am *not* going to school smelly because of you,' Poppy had said.

'People only wash in sinks in poor countries where they don't have showers,' Daisy pointed out. 'We have showers here, and they were invented to be used.'

Hope dried herself and then got dressed in old tracksuit bottoms, an old long-sleeved T-shirt that was too small for Daisy now, a hoodie and a fleece. It was going to be cold outside all day, so she needed layers.

She went back into the bedroom and sat down on her bed. She pulled out the park clean-up group sheet. She had divided the class into four groups of five. She'd put herself with Jayne and Katie and then Grace and Ivy too – they were nice and not annoying. She'd put Rebecca and Mina together with three other girls who were not enthusiastic about the clean-up day. Hope wasn't sure if Rebecca and Mina would even turn up. They said they were going to fake being sick so they didn't have to do her 'stupid project'. Hope wished they wouldn't come. It'd be much nicer without them. Mrs Lannigan was providing the bin bags, the high-vis vests and the pick-up sticks. Hope had given everyone a list of what to wear and bring in:

- *Thick rubber gloves or gardening gloves*

- *Long trousers/tracksuit and long-sleeved top – wear old clothes if possible*

- *Warm fleece*

- *Rainproof jacket*

- *Hat*

- *Old shoes/trainers or wellies*

- *Extra socks and shoes in case your feet get wet*

- *A sandwich/lunch*

- *Water*

- *Don't forget to wear a smile!*

Jayne had said she thought the last thing was a bit cheesy, but Hope wanted everyone to enjoy the day and get into it. She wanted to light a fire under the rest of her class so they'd start caring about saving the environment too.

Hope was too excited to wait around, so she packed her bag and headed into school early. It took her longer to walk there these days because she picked up every piece of rubbish she saw on the ground and put it in a bag, which she sorted out at school. There, she divided the rubbish into the recyclable or non-recyclable bins. Now, instead of it taking her twenty minutes to walk to school, it took thirty minutes. She just couldn't leave rubbish on the road, not when she knew that it caused so much harm to the environment.

Mrs Lannigan was already in the classroom, organising everything. She had only managed to get two pick-up sticks per group, so they'd have to take turns using them.

'That's OK, I'm happy to use my hands, I don't need a pick-up stick. In a way it's better if you bend down – you probably see more hidden rubbish that way,' Hope said.

Mrs Lannigan smiled at her. 'You're right, Hope, I'd say you do. I'm very impressed with how well you've organised everything and with your enthusiasm and commitment. You are an example to the rest of the class and your passion for this project is wonderful to see.'

Hope beamed. 'Thanks, I just think it's important that we all do our bit.'

'Well, you are doing a lot more than your bit, Hope. I'm very proud of you.'

Hope felt all warm inside. Mrs Lannigan was proud of her! And everyone knew that Mrs Lannigan didn't dish out praise easily.

One by one, Hope's classmates arrived. Most of them were wearing old tracksuits and warm jackets, but then Rebecca and Mina arrived.

'Seriously?' Katie whispered.

'What a joke.' Jayne snorted.

Hope just stared at them. Mina was wearing skinny pale pink jeans, bright white Fila trainers and a white sweatshirt. She was carrying a white fluffy fake-fur jacket over her arm.

Rebecca was wearing a cream minidress with the Balenciaga logo plastered across the front, silver tights and gold ankle boots. She had a leopard-print fur jacket slung over her arm. Hope wasn't even sure if it was fake fur or not. She prayed it was.

Mrs Lannigan looked the two girls up and down. 'Really and truly, what on earth are you wearing? Did you not read Hope's list? It clearly said old clothes and shoes.'

Rebecca flicked her hair. 'These *are* old clothes, Mrs Lannigan. I've had them for, like, two months.'

'Yeah, me too, really old,' Mina said.

'Oh really?' Jayne asked. 'Then how come there's a tag hanging out of the back of your sweatshirt, Mina?'

Mina's arm flew up to the back of her neck. She yanked

the tag off, going bright red as she did so. Everyone sniggered.

Mrs Lannigan rolled her eyes and then clapped her hands. 'Right, let's get going. We have lots of work to do. I'm hoping the rain will hold off, but we need to make the most of it while it's dry.'

Hope handed out the high-vis vests.

'Is this a joke?' Rebecca glared at her. 'There's no way I'm putting that disgusting thing on.'

'You have to,' Hope said.

'I don't *have* to do anything,' Rebecca snapped.

'It's the rule: we all have to wear these vests,' Hope reminded her.

'I don't care. I am not embarrassing myself with that revolting vest.'

'Rebecca!' Mrs Lannigan barked. 'Put that vest on this minute. I want no more nonsense from you. This is a clean-up, not a fashion show.'

'Like you'd know anything about fashion,' Rebecca hissed under her breath. Mina giggled.

Jayne accidentally-on-purpose bumped into Rebecca with her pick-up stick and laddered her silver tights.

'Oh my God, you idiot, these tights cost fifty euro!' Rebecca shrieked.

'Oops.' Jayne winked at Hope and Katie as they tried not to laugh out loud.

CHAPTER 16

Finally, they were ready to go. Hope led the way, while Mrs Lannigan and the sports teacher, Miss White, walked at the back of the line.

Hope could hear Rebecca moaning the whole way to the park.

'I thought you were going to pretend you were sick?' Mina was saying.

'I tried, obviously, but my cow of a mother made me come. I tried to get my dad to call the school and complain about child labour and get me out of it, but he said he was busy at work and didn't have time.'

'Same,' Mina said. 'My mum wouldn't let me stay at

home either. She gave me the whole "it's important to help others" speech. Like, who is this *actually* helping? No one. The park will be full of trash again tomorrow.'

'Totally,' Rebecca agreed. 'It's just stupid Hope and her pathetic save the world crap. My dad says it's all nonsense. He said the whole climate-change thing is just hippie freaks trying to make us all give up our sports cars and stop us flying anywhere and forcing us to eat rabbit food. He also said climate change is actually a good thing because we're getting longer, warmer summers.'

Hope tried to ignore Rebecca's whiny voice, but she just couldn't. She couldn't let Rebecca go around spreading total lies about the future of the world.

She spun around. 'Your dad is a big fat liar. The Earth's climate *is* getting warmer, but that means more droughts and more heatwaves. It's way harder to grow food if the soil is bone-dry. And the ice and snow are melting in the Arctic, meaning the sea levels are rising, so the beaches you want to go to will soon be gone!'

Rebecca pushed Hope in the chest. 'Don't you dare call my dad a liar. You're just a loser who goes around boring people about the planet. You sound like a teacher droning on and on. No one cares, don't you get it? No one here actually cares. We're not going to give up ice cream and cars and travelling. You're wasting your time and energy.'

'People do care,' Hope shouted back. 'Only ignorant people like you don't.'

'Really?' Rebecca sneered. 'Do you know what everyone in the class is saying about you? They all think you're a total freak. The only reason anyone agreed to this stupid outing is to get out of school. You're the thick one, Hope.'

'Leave Hope alone, you stupid cow,' Jayne chimed in. 'The only freak here is you, in your silver tights and ridiculous gold boots.'

Hope was grateful to Jayne for defending her, but Rebecca's words had stung. She looked around at her classmates. Was this day going to make them see what needed to be done? Would they start making changes in their lives to save the planet? Would this outing change anything? Or did they all think it was stupid, like Rebecca said?

Even Jayne and Katie weren't really invested. They did try a bit and had cut back on eating dairy and having long showers, but they still ate hamburgers and got lifts to school and they still used cling film to wrap their sandwiches, even though Hope had told them loads of times that cling film was super hard to recycle. She felt as if she was banging her head against a brick wall.

Hope was feeling pretty down in the dumps by the time they reached the park. But then Mrs Lannigan and Miss White came up to her and were all enthusiastic and asked her to help organise the bin bags and the pick-up sticks.

Everyone wanted to use the pick-up stick first so there was a bit of a tussle. The girls gathered in their groups and each group was given an area to clean up.

'Before we begin, I want to say a thank-you to Hope for coming up with this plan. She is a credit to the school and to herself,' Mrs Lannigan said.

The girls cheered – well, some of them did – and Hope felt a little better. *Change starts with baby steps*, she reminded herself for the millionth time.

When the teachers weren't looking, Rebecca grabbed the pick-up stick out of Laura's hand. 'I'll be taking that.'

Laura put a lump of her hair into her mouth and began to chew.

They went off in their groups, spread out all over the park. Hope was shocked at how much rubbish she found. Crisp packets, chocolate wrappers, tissues, leaflets, banana skins, apple cores, cling film, plastic sandwich wrappers, nappies (used stinky ones!), plastic bottles, cigarette butts … just *so much* rubbish.

'Oh my God! ARGHHHHHH!' Rebecca screamed.

Everyone turned from their groups to see what was going on.

Mrs Lannigan called over, 'What is it now, Rebecca?'

'Dog poo!' Rebecca roared. 'Disgusting dog poo and I stood on it. In my boots!' She started hyperventilating.

Hope, Jayne and Katie cracked up. 'Poo on her gold boots, I love it!' Jayne giggled.

'Serves her right for dressing in such ridiculous clothes,' Katie said.

'I am so over this.' Rebecca threw her pick-up stick on the ground. 'I am not picking up anyone else's rubbish. I am not a bin man. This whole thing is a disgrace. The school is going to have to pay for my boots,' she snapped.

Mrs Lannigan walked across the park and stood in front of her. 'Lower your voice, please, Rebecca. You are making a complete spectacle of yourself. You were told to wear old shoes, but you chose to wear those ridiculous boots. Every decision we make has consequences. Now go and sit on the bench over there, and I do not want to hear another word out of you.'

Rebecca stomped off to the bench. Hope watched as she took off her boot and tried to wipe the poo from the front of it with a tissue. But she just made it worse, spreading it all over. Rebecca hissed and cursed and stamped her other foot and eventually threw the smelly boot across the park.

It landed near where Hope's group was. Jayne, who had the pick-up stick, picked the boot up and put it in the bin bag, winking at the others.

They continued picking up rubbish for another hour and, slowly, the park began to look cleaner. Hope wanted to keep going, but everyone else had had enough and wanted a break.

Mrs Lannigan said they could have an early lunch and then do one more hour of cleaning.

There was a big groan. '*Another hour*?' people muttered. 'Haven't we done enough?' 'It's cold.' 'It's boring.' 'It's gross.' The complaints went on and on.

'Girls,' Mrs Lannigan said. 'The planet cannot be saved unless we all do our bit. Now, eat up and we'll start again in twenty minutes.'

The second half of the day was hard. Hope was totally focused, but no one else was. Everyone started chatting and messing. One group ended up splitting their bag and all of the rubbish fell out.

Jayne and Katie stood in the same spot chatting about who was the funniest character in *Modern Family*. Jayne said Haley was, but Katie thought it was Phil. Hope ignored them and kept picking up rubbish. Her back was sore and her hands were cold, but she kept on going.

When Mrs Lannigan told them all that they could pack up and go, Hope asked if she could stay.

'I'm sorry, Hope, I can't leave you here. We've done a good job – the park is probably cleaner than it has been in years. We filled ten bin bags. You should be proud of yourself.'

But Hope wasn't proud. She was frustrated, because there was still rubbish around. They hadn't picked up all of it, but Mrs Lannigan was firm: Hope was not allowed to stay in the park alone.

They set off back for school. Jayne handed Rebecca back her poo-covered boot, which Rebecca put in an empty bag, then shoved it in Mina's backpack. Mina looked grossed out but said nothing. Rebecca was also wearing Mina's spare pair of shoes – brand-new white Adidas trainers with rose-gold stripes. They were much too small for Rebecca, but she wore them anyway.

'Maybe someone else has trainers in your size?' Mina

said hopefully, looking at her new runners being ruined by Rebecca's big feet.

Rebecca glared at her. 'I don't want to wear anyone else's disgusting shoes. What's the big deal?'

Mina shuffled from one foot to the other. 'Well, it's just that you're squashing the backs down and they're brand new.'

'I have to push the backs down – they're too small. Your feet are, like, baby size. Who cares? They're not even that nice anyway.'

Mina stood and watched as Rebecca strode off, using her new trainers as flip-flops.

'I almost feel sorry for Mina,' Jayne whispered, watching them.

'If she wasn't such a cow, maybe, but actually, it's kind of karma,' Katie said.

Maybe Mina would finally see what a selfish and mean person Rebecca was, Hope thought. Maybe this would open her eyes to the fact that Rebecca was a rotten friend to her. She wouldn't bet on it, though.

They trudged back to school, carrying their bags of rubbish.

CHAPTER 17

Hope sat in the kitchen, her hands wrapped around a hot chocolate. Mum used to say that you shouldn't drink hot chocolate first thing in the morning because it was too much sugar on an empty stomach, but some of her rules had died with her. Anyway, it was Saturday and even Mum had allowed treats on the weekend. Hope had made her hot chocolate with almond milk, so it didn't taste like the ones Mum used to make, but Hope was getting used to the taste of almond milk and liked it now.

She was looking out the window at the blue sky and the winter frost covering their little back garden. A robin hopped along the wall and the sun began to melt the frost away. It was so pretty and peaceful.

The door was flung open. Poppy stood in the doorway, her duvet wrapped around her. 'What the hell is going on? It's like the North Pole in this house. Is the heating broken?'

Hope said nothing. She wasn't going to admit that she'd changed the timer. Dad set the heat to come on from six to nine in the morning and from five to ten at night. But they didn't need it in the mornings. If they could cut out those three hours of heat every morning, they would be using way less energy every day.

'Where's Dad?' Poppy asked.

'He went to get the newspaper and a coffee.'

'Didn't he notice that the house is like an igloo?' Poppy demanded.

'Actually, igloos can be warm. The temperature outside an igloo could be as low as minus forty-five degrees but inside the igloo it could be up to sixteen degrees.'

Poppy stared at her little sister. 'Do you honestly think I want a lecture on stupid igloos? What I *want* is for someone to fix the heating, so I don't freeze to death.'

Daisy came in wearing a coat, hat and scarf over her pyjamas. 'What's going on? It's freezing.'

'I'll make you hot chocolates – it'll warm you up,' Hope offered.

Poppy narrowed her eyes. 'Why are you so fine about the house being like an ice cube?'

Hope busied herself getting two mugs out and filling them with chocolate powder and cow's milk. She knew they'd kick up a stink if she gave them almond.

'Aren't you cold?' Daisy asked.

'Of course she is, she's wearing her furry fleece,' Poppy pointed out.

Daisy's eyes widened. 'Oh my God, Hope, did you do something to the heating?'

Hope froze. Thank goodness she had her back to her sisters so they couldn't see her guilty face.

'Did you turn the heating off?' Poppy said accusingly.

Mum always said it was wrong to lie, but Hope also wanted to come out of this conversation alive.

'I just woke up and it was cold.' She shrugged. It was the truth; she *had* woken up and the house *was* freezing. She'd just left out the bit about sneaking downstairs when everyone was asleep and changing the timer.

'I thought it might be another one of your "torture your family while trying to save the world" things,' Poppy said.

Hope handed them both mugs of hot chocolate.

'Yum,' Daisy said.

'Thanks.' Poppy sipped her chocolate.

The front door opened and Dad came in. He put his paper on the table and went to take off his coat, then stopped.

'Has the heating not come on yet?'

Poppy waved her duvet at him. 'Obviously not. *Please* fix it, Dad.'

Dad went out to the little boiler room and came back in frowning. 'That's odd, the morning timer was turned off.'

'Who turned it off? Was it you, Hope?' Daisy said, turning on her.

Hope gave a little shake of her head, fingers crossed behind her back.

'I bet it was, you liar!' Poppy shouted.

Dad gave Hope a sideways glance. 'No, I think it just does that sometimes, there's a glitch in the timer. Anyway, it's on again now. We'll be warm in no time.'

The twins shuffled out of the kitchen and back up to their bedroom to snuggle under their duvets until the heat kicked in.

'Hope?'

'We don't need the heat on in the morning.'

'Yes, we do. It's winter, Hope, it's freezing. You'll all get sick if you wake up to a freezing cold house every morning,' Dad said.

'Germs make you sick, not cold weather,' Hope explained.

'Hope, you have to stop, love. You're going too far. I understand you want to do your bit to help battle climate change, but you can't make us all freeze to death in the process. You should be out having fun with your friends, not obsessing about the ozone layer and recycling. It's too much, you're consumed by it. I'm worried about you – you need to stop now. I want you to take a break from it all. Why don't you invite Jayne and Katie over and have a sleepover and watch a movie and eat sweets and forget about the planet for a while? OK?'

'No, it's not OK. If we forget about it for a while we'll never solve the problem,' Hope said.

'Hope, I am your father and I'm telling you to take a break from it.'

Hope shrugged and left the room. He didn't understand. He didn't care. No one in her family cared and because of that, *she* had to care even more, and work even harder.

CHAPTER 18

Hope woke up on her twelfth birthday and felt like a big rock was pushing down on her chest. It was her first birthday without Mum. She had died shortly after Hope's eleventh birthday. The twentieth of November last year was the day Hope's heart broke. But even though she had been really sick, Mum had still managed to make Hope's birthday perfect. She had been the best birthday organiser ever.

On the day of every birthday that Hope could remember, Mum had been the first person into her bedroom. She'd tiptoe in and wake Hope up by covering her face with kisses and telling her how much she loved her and what fun they were going to have. Hope was always already awake but pretending she wasn't. She never slept properly the night before her birthday. She'd lie awake full of excitement about the day ahead. She'd nod off for a bit here and there, but she always woke up really early and lay awake listening for the sound of her mum opening her bedroom door and creeping in. Hope would close her eyes and wait for the lovely warm kisses.

Mum would tell Hope to stay in bed while she got all the final preparations ready. But Hope always sat at the top of the stairs in her dressing gown, listening to the sounds of Mum getting everything organised, telling Dad and the twins to help with plates and candles.

Hope would sit there, her heart racing with excitement, then, after what seemed like ages but was probably only ten minutes, Mum would call her down. Hope would race into the kitchen and fling open the door.

The whole place would be covered in birthday banners and balloons. The table would have the special Happy Birthday tablecloth on it and all of her presents would be piled up in the middle, wrapped in shiny gold paper with red or silver bows. Mum had been the best present-wrapper in the whole world.

Hope's presents were never super fancy or expensive, because Mum said they had to spend the money they had on important things like schoolbooks and paying the mortgage for the house, and buying car insurance, and all that stuff. But still, she always managed to get Hope brilliant presents. She bought lots of little things, so the pile looked really big. Hope would sit at the end of the table and Dad would put a birthday crown on her head.

Then, Mum would bring over the cake. Every year it was the same, Hope's favourite – chocolate biscuit cake with marshmallows and Maltesers inside and the whole top covered in Smarties. It was the best cake in the whole wide world. It looked amazing, all the different-coloured Smarties were like a rainbow of colour, and it tasted even better. Hope would blow out her candles and Mum would tell her to make a wish. Then she would cut a huge piece and hand it to the birthday girl to scoff down.

Hope would then open her presents one by one. When it was the twins' birthday, they would rip open their presents, chucking the paper and bows aside without thinking, eager to see what was inside, but Hope liked to open her gifts slowly, one by one, carefully unwrapping the paper. Poppy and Daisy always complained that she was too slow and tried to hurry her along, but she liked to make the special moment last as long as possible.

Hope knew this birthday would be different. Very different. Even though Mum was sick on her last birthday, she'd still organised everything to be the same. Nothing today would be the same. Nothing on any of her birthdays from now on would ever be the same.

Hope could hear voices outside in the corridor. Her sisters were trying to whisper, but they were not doing a good job of it: she could hear them clearly.

'What do you mean, you forgot the Smarties? For goodness' sake, Mum always had Smarties on top. It's going to look crap without the Smarties and you made it all lopsided. It looks rubbish,' Daisy hissed.

'Sod off,' Poppy snapped. 'It's not that easy to make a perfect cake and I just forgot the Smarties.'

'It was the only thing you had to do. I had to get the presents and wrap them all.'

'You only bought two presents. Dad gave you the other two. All you had to do was throw some wrapping paper around them, big deal!'

'Well, all *you* did was make the cake and it's totally uneven,' Daisy snapped back.

'Yeah, well, you got crap presents.'

'Next year you can get them, then. It's not easy to buy a bunch of presents with only twenty euro.'

'Girls, be quiet. You'll wake Hope up before we're ready,' Dad whisper-shouted.

Hope heard them go downstairs and then she heard a roar, a lot of shouting and blaming and cursing.

Eventually, sick of waiting, she got up and went down to the kitchen.

'You bumped my arm,' Poppy was shouting.

'No, you crashed into *me*,' Daisy roared back.

'The cake is ruined.'

'It looked rubbish anyway.'

'Stop being such a cow,' Poppy snapped.

'I'm being honest. You're not exactly a contender for *The Great British Bake-Off*.'

'Fine,' Poppy shouted. 'Next year *you* can make the stupid cake.'

'GIRLS!' Dad raised his voice to be heard. 'Stop bickering. It's Hope's birthday, and we need to make it nice for her.'

Hope opened the door and stood in the doorway observing the mess. Poppy was crouched down, scooping a smashed chocolate biscuit cake off the floor. Daisy was trying to hang up a Happy Birthday banner, but it kept falling down, and Dad was blowing up balloons, his face bright red.

Daisy was the first to spot her.

'Noooooo!' She ran to close the door. 'We're not ready, it's a disaster. We need more time.'

Hope pushed the door back. 'It's OK. It was never going to be the same anyway.'

Dad tied a knot in his balloon and placed it on the table beside four other coloured balloons. Two of them had shrivelled up – he clearly hadn't tied the knots properly.

Poppy scooped the ruined cake onto a plate. 'Ta-da!' She tried to laugh it off. 'I realise it looks awful, but hopefully it'll taste nice.'

'It looks like a dog came in, vomited all over the floor and you put it onto a plate,' Daisy said.

Dad led Hope to the chair at the head of the kitchen table. He put the party crown on her head. Hope didn't feel in a party mood, but she tried to play along.

Poppy placed the lump of mushed cake in front of her and stuck a few candles into it. Dad pulled a lighter out of his pocket and lit them.

'Make a wish,' he said.

Hope closed her eyes and blew. *I wish Mum was here. I wish Mum hadn't died. I wish our family didn't have a big hole where Mum used to be. She was the centre, she was the glue, she was our everything. I wish my mum was alive.*

Hope knew it was a wasted wish because people couldn't come back from the dead, but it was what she wanted most in the world, apart from to save the planet, so that was what she wished for.

She opened her eyes and Daisy plonked four presents in front of her. The gifts were wrapped in plain blue wrapping paper and drowning in Sellotape. The wrapping paper was all scrunched at the ends. There were no bows this year.

'I know I did a rubbish job. Mum was the queen of wrapping, but I tried,' Daisy admitted.

'It's fine, thanks.' Hope tried to be nice and also not to mind the use of wrapping paper that was not recyclable. She opened the first gift. It was a light blue sweatshirt that she'd said she liked when she was out with the twins. Daisy had remembered; that was nice. The next package was a sparkly red notebook and pen.

'It's for you to write all your boring facts and figures about climate and eco-whatever in,' Daisy explained.

'Thanks, I love them.' Hope hugged her sisters. She could see they had made an effort and she wanted to show that she was grateful.

The next present was a box of sweets – Heroes – from Dad.

'Because you're my little hero,' he said, his eyes shining with tears.

Hope looked away. She knew she'd start crying too if she didn't.

The last gift was a small one. Hope took ages to unwrap it because Daisy had wrapped half a roll of Sellotape around it. Eventually, she managed to get the wrapping off using a pair of scissors. Under the paper was a small black box. She flipped it open and inside was a pair of slim, delicate, gold hoop earrings.

She looked up at her dad. 'But ...'

He smiled at her sadly. 'Mum wanted you to have them. She told me to give them to you on your twelfth birthday.'

Hope felt a big lump in her throat. They were Mum's favourite earrings. She had worn them all the time. They *were* Mum. They were a part of her. They were so special. It was like she was here in the room with them.

Hope didn't realise she was crying until Poppy handed her a tissue. She was crying too, as was Daisy.

'Thank you,' Hope croaked and hugged Dad. He hugged her back and wiped a tear from his own cheek.

There was silence in the kitchen until Daisy said, 'OK, no more crying. So, Dad, what did Mum tell you to give *us* on our next birthday? Did she leave me her diamond ring? Oh, I hope she did. I really want that.'

'Hey, *I* want that,' Poppy said. 'You can have her silver bracelet.'

'No way, I'm getting the diamond. She preferred me to you.'

'No, she did not!' Poppy said. 'I was her favourite because I looked like her.'

Hope put the earrings into her ears. She felt her earlobes warm up. It felt like Mum was kissing her ears. A warm glow lit up inside her.

While the twins argued over who was Mum's favourite and Dad tried to stop them, Hope touched her earrings and smiled. She knew she was Mum's favourite; she always had been. The twins could shout all they wanted and could have Mum's diamond ring if they wished. Hope had got the items that Mum wore every day, her favourite jewellery. The earrings meant the world to her. They were just like Mum – classic and elegant. Not showy or fancy, just really pretty and simple.

The birthday Hope had been dreading had turned out OK. Even though Mum was no longer with them, Hope knew that she had been thinking about her, and that made her so happy.

CHAPTER 19

One morning a couple of days later, Hope was sorting the family's recycling when Poppy came downstairs and stopped dead at the kitchen door.

'Oh my God, we've been robbed!' she shrieked.

'What?' Daisy came in behind her.

'Quick, run, the robber could still be here – he could murder us.' Poppy shoved Daisy out of the way and ran to the front door.

'Poppy!' Daisy shouted after her twin. 'We haven't been robbed, it's just our freak little sister.'

Poppy came back into the kitchen. 'What?'

149

Daisy pointed to Hope, who was sitting in the corner of the kitchen, slightly hidden by the bin, surrounded by rubbish.

'What on earth are you doing?' Poppy demanded.

'Sorting out our rubbish,' Hope said, her face red with effort. 'I found this!' She shook a fluffy sock in the air.

'So?' Daisy asked, hands on hips.

'So,' Hope hissed, 'you cannot put clothes in the green bin. It's only for dry and loose paper and plastic.'

'I thought you could recycle clothes.'

'You can, but they have to go into the clothes bank. And who put this in?' Hope waved a Styrofoam container in the air.

'I did,' Poppy said. 'There was a big fat juicy burger in it and it tasted delicious. I don't care about cow farts – I like burgers and I'm not giving them up for your revolting chickpea mushy fake burgers.'

'I've told you before, Styrofoam takes five hundred years to break down!' Hope shouted.

'I don't care,' Poppy said. 'I am sick of being dragged out of the shower, told not to flush the loo, frozen in my own house and constantly having no battery on my phone

150

because you keep unplugging the charger. I'm sick of *you*, Hope.'

'Me too, you've become a pain in the face,' Daisy agreed.

Hope stood up and shook a lump of cling film at them. 'Well, I've had enough of you not caring about anyone or anything but yourselves. It's people like you who are destroying the world. You're so selfish.'

'You're the one ruining our lives,' Daisy snapped back.

'Seriously, Hope, it's getting really annoying now. We're sick of it.' Poppy agreed with her twin.

'Well, I'm sick of *you*,' Hope muttered, as she continued to sort out the recycling. 'I'm going to be late for school because of this. Why can't you stop criticising me and just help me!' she roared.

She really was fed up with her sisters. They weren't making any effort. They still had long showers and ignored the timer buzzing to tell them to stop. They still flushed the toilet all the time. They still put the heat on too often and too high. They still left their phones plugged in all night long, and they still ate red meat and dairy all the time.

Nothing had changed, even though Hope had tried so hard to persuade them. She was getting sick and tired of not getting through to her own family. If she couldn't even persuade *them* to change, what chance did she have of persuading anyone else? What chance did the world have?

Everything was horrible. Life sucked. Mum's anniversary was coming up and Hope felt sick about it. Dad hadn't mentioned it, and she was scared he'd forgotten because he was so busy with work and Janice and trying to keep the twins out of trouble. Hope wanted them to spend the day together, talking about Mum and looking at photos and videos and remembering her. She hated that no one talked about her; she hated that Mum was being forgotten.

Later that morning at school, Hope was at the back of the group as they ran around the playing field. She was one of the slowest runners in her class. She hated athletics. She liked tennis and basketball, but running was a pain. Her legs were aching and she wanted to stop, but Miss White made you do extra laps if you stopped. Hope was feeling fed up. It felt as if no one was listening to her, no one cared about the environment.

In front of her, Rebecca and Mina were going equally slowly.

'Are you dying to see your baby sister?' Mina asked.

'Oh yeah, totally. I'll be going over soon to see her.'

'When?'

'I don't know exactly.' Rebecca scowled. 'Olga says I have to wait until Starlight is a bit older to come and visit. She's being, like, totally over-protective.'

'Starlight is such an amazing name. It's, like, a total celebrity name.'

'No, it isn't. Rebecca is way more of a celebrity name.'

'I guess so ...' Mina muttered. 'Have you seen photos? Is she beautiful like Olga?'

'She's a tiny bald baby, Mina, she's not even that cute.'

Hope smiled to herself. Rebecca was clearly not happy about her new sister.

'Anyway, it's not all about Starlight. I do have a big birthday of my own coming up soon, you know.'

'OMG, of course, as if I'd forget that. Any idea what presents you're getting?'

'Well, obviously turning twelve is, like, a really big deal and both my parents know that.'

'Yeah, totally.' Mina puffed as she tried to talk and jog.

'So, I'm getting an electric scooter, a whole set of MAC make-up brushes and eyeshadows and lip glosses, these amazing black Prada boots and a backpack to match, an

Apple Watch from my dad, and new AirPods and these really cool Fendi sunglasses.'

'Wow, you have seriously cool presents – you're so lucky,' Mina gushed.

'Yeah, well, my parents are minted, so they should buy me cool stuff. My mum always gets me other little things like silk pyjamas and clothes, as well.'

Hope felt a bit jealous of all Rebecca's amazing presents until she remembered Mum's earrings. She wasn't allowed to wear hoop earrings in school, only little stud ones, so she could only wear Mum's on the weekends, but still, they meant more than all of Rebecca's gifts.

'Only two weeks to go until you get all that stuff,' Mina noted.

'I'll probably get lots of it before my actual birthday. My dad's secretary is sending it all over. He's super busy with work and Olga is being even more needy since Starlight was born. She won't let my dad leave her side. Like, it's just a stupid baby and they have a nanny. It's the first time Dad's going to miss my birthday.' Rebecca's voice shook with emotion. 'I hate Olga, she ruins everything.'

Ouch. Hope could tell Rebecca was really hurt that her dad was missing her birthday.

Mina began to run even more slowly, clutching her side. 'I suppose all new mums are a bit nervous. It's so cool to have a little sister, though. You can look after her and babysit her and stuff.'

Rebecca glared at Mina. '*Hello!* I'm not a nanny. There is no way I'm babysitting anyone. Anyway, she's only my half-sister and if she turns out anything like her mother, she'll be a pain.'

Hope slowed down. She didn't want to pass them now. *That poor little baby*, she thought, *to end up with an older sister like Rebecca. She's lucky she lives in a different country.*

'Is your mum still going out with Hope's dad?' Mina obviously wanted to change the subject.

'Oh my God, unfortunately, yes. But it won't last, Mum will get bored with him soon.'

'I hope so, for your sake,' Mina said. 'So you won't have to sit through any more dinners with Hope. She's so weird and annoying. She'd better not organise any more save the world activities – that one in the park was horrendous. My trainers were ruined.'

Rebecca snorted. 'Even her own father can't stand her. I heard him telling my mum what a pain Hope is to live with. He said she's driving them all crazy with her environmental crap. He said he's worried about her, that her obsession isn't normal and that he's going to take her to see a therapist. He asked my mum if she'd heard of any good ones.'

'Oh my God, so even her family hate her!' Mina giggled.

'Hardly surprising, imagine having to live with that – *ewwwww*.' Rebecca turned up her nose and they both cracked up laughing.

Hope stopped running. She stood completely still, watching the two girls jog off. Trembling, she walked over to a bush and vomited. She vomited up her disappointment and her feeling of being betrayed by her own dad.

She wiped her mouth with the sleeve of her sweatshirt. How could he? How could Dad talk about her like that to Janice? How could the man who hugged her and called her his hero betray her like that? How could he be so cruel? Did he really think she was mad? Was he going to make her see a therapist?

Hope began to sob. All she wanted was to make the world a better place. Mum would have been proud of her, and she'd thought Dad would be too. She'd thought he understood what she was trying to do. Hope's whole body shook as she cried and cried. Her heart was broken. Her lovely dad was telling people she was a pain. He had let her down in the worst way. She hated him for it. Hope sobbed until there were no more tears to cry.

When she had calmed down a little, she walked out of the school gate and went home. It was only eleven in the morning, but she didn't care about skipping school. She needed to go home and figure out what to do. What *do* you do when your family hates you and thinks you're weird, strange and annoying? Where do you go? Who do you turn to? How do you find a way to feel less alone?

Hope walked along the road feeling helpless. But then, suddenly, it came to her. She had the solution. It was right in front of her.

There was only one person in the world who would get it. Who could understand what she was going through and help her. And Hope was going to find her.

CHAPTER 20

Hope pulled the hidden key out from under the flowerpot and opened the front door. The house was quiet. She went up to her bedroom and started to pull all of her clothes out onto the bed.

Her phone rang. It was Dad.

'Hi, the school just rang – they said you were seen leaving the grounds. Are you OK?'

Yeah, like you care about me, Hope thought. *Like you actually give a damn about my life or my feelings.*

'I'm fine, I just vomited after running and wanted to come home and lie down.'

The getting sick part was true, but the reason wasn't. Then again, Hope wasn't about to tell her dad that she had vomited because he was a traitor who was mean and nasty about her behind her back.

'Oh my goodness, Hope, are you OK?'

'I'm fine, I just need to sleep for a bit.'

'I'll come home.'

'No,' Hope was firm. 'I just need to rest. I'm totally fine.'

'Do you think it was something you ate?'

'No, we just had to run for ages and it made me feel sick. I hate running.'

'OK, pet, have a rest and call me when you wake up so I know you're OK.'

'I will. I'm going to lie down now.'

'Mind yourself, love you.'

Hope hung up. She was not going to say 'I love you' back. No way. She looked at her clothes. She'd have to fit everything into a backpack. She only needed important things – two pairs of jeans, two warm fleeces, a rain jacket, two pairs of trainers, seven pairs of socks and pants, four T-shirts, a toothbrush, a small tube of toothpaste, a hairbrush, a bar of soap, earphones and a book to read. They were the practical things she needed. Now she focused on the things that were most important to her. She took out her stud earrings and put on Mum's gold hoops. She pulled the Coco Mademoiselle perfume out from under her pillow and packed that in the front pouch of her backpack, along with the two precious photos of her and Mum.

Hope zipped up her backpack and headed downstairs to the kitchen, where the computer was set up in the corner. She started googling.

It was all very well deciding to go to meet your hero, but first you had to figure out how to get there. Stockholm was in Sweden. That was where Greta lived. *OK,* Hope thought, *I'll go to Sweden. But how?*

She googled 'cheapest way to get from Dublin to Stockholm'.

The cheapest and quickest way turned out to be flying, but Hope knew flying was bad for the environment – hadn't Greta sailed all the way to America for a conference, rather than flying? She couldn't show up to see her hero off the plane! Anyway, she didn't think they'd let a kid on a plane with no parents. She'd have to get buses and trains and boats. They'd be easier to sneak on and off of.

Hope kept searching. There was a bus that went from Dublin to Stockholm via London, Lille and Hamburg. The whole journey took about forty-six hours and the website said it would cost about one hundred euro.

Hope ran upstairs to raid her piggy bank. She pulled the bottom off and shook the pig. Coins fell out and then a ten-euro note. Hope counted up all the money she had in the world: €18.67. She would not let herself give up. She went into the twins' room and began to go through all their drawers.

She found €15 in Poppy's bedside locker, hidden in her jewellery box. Daisy's locker had no money in it. Hope went through their clothes drawers. Bingo! In Daisy's sock drawer, hidden at the back, was a small zip-up purse. Hope opened it and found €50.

She knew it was wrong to take her sisters' money, but this was an emergency. She'd pay them back somehow.

OK, so now she had €83.67. She needed more for the trip. She went into Dad's room and rummaged around. She found €5 in his bedside drawer and €10 in one of his jacket pockets. Now she had €98.67. She went downstairs and went through the pockets of all the coats hanging up. She found €4.80 in loose change. Now she had enough, €103.47.

Hope went back upstairs and put all the money carefully into a small purse. She changed out of her sports kit and pulled on her jeans, T-shirt, fleece, socks and trainers. She carefully put her purse deep into the front pocket of her jeans. She could not lose that money.

Then Hope sat down and wrote out her travel plan. She was going to get a bus from Dublin that went on a boat to Wales and then by road to London. That would take about twelve hours. She would arrive in Victoria Station, where she would then get another bus that went from London to Lille. Hope googled Lille – it was in France. That journey would take six hours. Then in Lille, Hope would have to change buses and get on one going to Hamburg. Hope had to google Hamburg too – it was in Germany. This journey would take ten and a half hours. In Hamburg, she had to change again and get one last bus from Hamburg to Stockholm. That would take fourteen hours and twenty minutes.

Hope wrote everything down. All the details of the bus stations and the changes and the transfers and the time it would take. It was scary, but it was what she had to do. She had no choice. She couldn't stay here where everyone hated her. She had to go and find Greta and talk to her and maybe she could stay with Greta's family. They understood the importance of doing everything possible to prevent climate change. They wouldn't think she was a freak. They wouldn't talk about her behind her back. They wouldn't make her feel so alone and hurt.

Hope took out the bread and set about making herself a large batch of sandwiches for her big journey. Forty-six hours was nearly two whole days. Hope made four big sandwiches filled with hummus and vegan cheese. Then she packed three apples, two bananas and three bars of Nobó vegan chocolate, the orange flavour one, which was her favourite. Finally, she filled up her big water bottle with water and shoved it into the net pouch on the side of her backpack.

She had to write down the directions to the bus station because her rubbish phone didn't have Google Maps.

Hope pulled on her coat, gloves and hat, and put her passport into the inside pocket of her coat. She was ready.

Before she left, she sat down to write a note:

You all hate me and think I'm weird and a freak for caring about the environment. I can't live here anymore. Mum would have understood, but she's gone, so I've gone to find the only other person in the world who will understand me.

Goodbye,

Hope.

Hope didn't feel one bit sad. She was glad she was getting away from her horrible family. She was happy to be going to meet her hero. Maybe when Greta met her and saw how into saving the planet she was, they'd become best friends and Greta could be like a big sister to her. A much better one than Daisy and Poppy. Hope could work with her and help her with her activism. She'd be appreciated, not made fun of.

No one would be laughing at her when they saw her on YouTube making big important speeches side by side with Greta. Dad wouldn't think Hope was an annoying pain then. He'd realise that he should be proud of her and that she was right and he should have listened to her.

Hope picked up her rucksack and walked out of the door. She put the key back under the flowerpot and walked through the gate and down the road.

Stockholm, here I come!

CHAPTER 21

H ope arrived at the main bus station in Dublin after an hour and a half of walking, following the directions she'd written out. She stared at the ticket machine. She tried to figure out how to pay for her ticket to London. It was better to buy it at a machine than at the counter: a machine couldn't ask her questions about why she was travelling alone and ask where her parents were.

She followed the instructions and eventually figured it out. A ticket dropped into the bottom of the machine. Hope was on her way!

She knew from watching movies that if a kid was travelling alone and didn't want to be spotted by nosy adults or the police, they needed to look like they were with a family. Hope spotted a family of five: a mum, dad and three kids. The kids looked a bit younger than her, but not so much that she couldn't be their sister. When it came to boarding the bus, Hope walked up with the family and the man checking the tickets presumed they were all together. *Phew!*

She sat down in the row behind the family and plugged in her earphones. She played the few basic games her old phone had and listened to some music. Now that she was on the bus, her stomach was doing little flips. Some of it was excitement, but mostly it was nerves.

Hope was on her way to Stockholm, but she didn't actually have an address for Greta. It hadn't come up when she'd searched on Google, but Hope was sure that everyone in Stockholm would know where she lived. It was like the king in England – everyone knew he lived in Buckingham Palace. Greta was the most famous person in Sweden, so everyone would definitely know where she lived.

Hope decided to eat one sandwich and half of a chocolate bar. The food settled her stomach as the bus drove onto the boat.

When they parked on the boat, everyone got off the bus and wandered upstairs to the deck. It was full of restaurants, cafés and big open lounge spaces, and everywhere was crammed with people. The boat reminded Hope of the one they'd taken on their family trip to France the year before Mum got sick. They'd driven over to stay in a campsite and had the best time. Hope pushed the memory away. It was too painful, and she had to stay focused now.

She followed the family and watched as they headed to the main restaurant. She stopped at the entrance, smelling all the lovely hot food. But she only had enough money for her travel tickets, so she found a seat in the main lounge area of the boat and curled up in a seat, trying to look invisible.

She allowed herself to eat the second half of the bar of chocolate as a treat. All around her, families were having picnics and young kids were running around, shouting and spilling drinks on the ground. Different groups of young men and women were sitting playing cards, drinking beer, taking selfies and laughing. To her left a big group of teenagers were sitting in a circle, chatting and having fun. They were all wearing tracksuits with 'Johnstown Football' across the back. A team off to play a match in the UK. Hope used to think of her family as a team; Mum had called them 'Team Dillon'. But they weren't a team anymore, because when their captain died their team fell apart. They didn't support each other or have each other's backs like a real team did.

Hope suddenly felt very alone. But that was because she *was* alone. Her family didn't like her or understand her. Even Jayne and Katie had asked her to stop talking about climate change all the time because it was getting a 'bit boring'. Mum would have listened. Mum would have helped her. She'd never have betrayed her like Dad had. Never. Hope didn't think she'd ever be able to forgive him. The fact that he'd said it to Janice, Rebecca's mum, was the worst. Hope felt teary just thinking about it. She closed her eyes and tried to block out the pain. The gentle rocking of the boat soothed her and soon she was fast asleep, her head on her arm.

CHAPTER 22

While Hope was sailing across the Irish Sea, at home everyone was going crazy. Her dad, Joe, had come home from work early, worried when Hope didn't answer her phone. He went upstairs and saw clothes and mess all over her bedroom. He checked the twins' room and saw all the drawers open, then the same thing in his own bedroom. He ran downstairs into the kitchen – and that's when he saw the note.

Joe thought he was having a heart attack. The words began to swim in front of his eyes and he fell sideways into a chair. *Oh my God, where's Hope? Where has my baby girl gone? Why does she think we all hate her?*

'I've gone to find the only other person in the world who will understand me'

Who was the only other person in the world who understood her? Joe's head throbbed and his heart raced in his chest. Maybe the twins would know what Hope meant. He got back into the car and raced over to their school.

Joe followed the principal into the twins' classroom. They both looked up.

'Excuse the interruption, but Poppy and Daisy need to grab their bags and leave immediately,' said the principal.

Daisy looked at Joe. 'What's going on?'

'I'll explain in the car. Just hurry up.'

The twins threw their books into their backpacks and hurried after their dad. Joe strode down the corridor and out the front door of the school. The twins ran behind him.

'Look, Dad, we didn't mean to forge the note, we're sorry. We just didn't have time to study for the maths test, so we thought it was best if we pretended to be sick,' Daisy said.

'We know it was wrong, we won't do it again,' Poppy said.

Joe slowed down and turned to face them. 'What are you talking about?'

'Well, the note ... I mean, isn't that why ...' Daisy said.

'Are we grounded?' Poppy asked. 'We promise—'

Joe cut across Poppy. 'Hope's gone.'

'What?' The twins looked at each other.

'Her phone is dead, and she left a note saying she knows we all hate her and she's gone to see the one person who'll understand her. Who is she talking about? What is going on?' Joe's voice came out all high and shaky.

'She's probably just looking for attention,' Daisy said.

'Yeah, she's probably gone to pick up trash in the park,' Poppy said. 'Maybe she means the park ranger or the bin man understands her, or something.'

Joe frowned. 'I don't think so. The whole house is turned upside down. She took money from my room and it looks like she's taken some of her clothes as well.'

'She'd better not have taken my money,' Daisy said.

Joe handed them Hope's note. They both read it.

'This is so typical of Hope. She's such a drama queen. I bet she's hiding somewhere trying to freak us out because

171

we're flushing the loo and taking showers that last longer than two minutes,' Poppy said.

Joe shook his head. 'I think it's more than that, girls. I think she really feels alone. I'm worried. I need you to look in her room and see if you can tell me what's missing. I know she's taken her trainers and her big red fleece, and she seems to be missing socks and pants.'

'If she gave my money to some hippie-dippie cause, I'll kill her.' Daisy scowled.

Joe glared at her. 'Daisy,' he snapped, 'your sister is missing. We have more important things to be worrying about than your money.'

'Keep your hair on, Dad, I bet she'll be back home by dinner time to annoy us all with her vegan food,' Poppy said.

When they got home, Daisy raced upstairs to check her money. Joe and Poppy followed her up.

'Oh my God, she stole all my savings!'

'How much was it?' Joe asked.

'Fifty euro, and it took me ages and ages to save it.' Daisy was clearly upset. 'She's going to pay me back, plus interest, the little cow.'

'She took fifteen euro from my drawer too,' Poppy said.

'I'm missing a few euro as well. All together it's a lot of money.' Joe rubbed his eyes. 'Who do you think she's going to see? Who could she mean? Who's the only person in the world who will understand her?'

Daisy sat on her bed holding her now-empty purse. 'Well, she's obsessed with that dorky girl with the plaits. Greta whatshername.'

Joe's head snapped up. 'Oh my God, that's it. That's exactly who she means. She's gone to see Greta Thunberg.'

'There's no way she's gone to find her. She lives in, like, Norway or something,' Daisy said.

'Sweden, I think,' Joe said, looking concerned.

'Is that where Greta lives? I'd love to go to Sweden. The guys are supposed to be really fit.'

'Soooo good-looking,' Poppy agreed.

Joe thumped his hand down on the chest of drawers. 'Girls! This is not a laughing matter. Your sister is missing. She could be halfway to Sweden by now. THIS IS REALLY SERIOUS!'

'Sorry, Dad,' Daisy said, evidently realising how worried he was. 'Did you try calling her again?'

'Obviously, yes. Her phone's dead.'

'Do you think we should call the police?' Daisy asked.

'Yes, I'm going to do that now, and I want you to call her friends too. They should be home from school by now.'

'I'll call Jayne, I have her number, and she can call Katie and all the others,' Poppy said.

'You should call Janice too, Dad,' Daisy suggested. 'Rebecca's in her class – she might know something.'

'Good idea.'

Don't freak out, Dad, it's only four o'clock. She can't have got that far, surely?' Poppy said.

'Let's hope not,' Joe said.

'Do you think she's going to fly there?' Daisy asked.

'I don't think they'd let a kid on a plane without a parent,' Poppy noted.

'Maybe she's getting the boat? It's probably easier to sneak on.' Daisy said.

'*Is* there a boat to Sweden?' Poppy asked.

Joe swallowed back the panic building inside him. 'I need to figure all that out. Hopefully the police will help.'

'I hope she's OK. I mean ... she must have been feeling really bad to run away,' Daisy was concerned now too.

Poppy put her hand on her father's shoulder. 'Let's be real. Hope would never run away, Dad. She doesn't even like being in the house on her own for an hour. I reckon she'll be back soon. She's just messing with us. She's probably gone shopping for green food and left the note to shock us into listening to her climate stuff. I think that when she comes back we should support her more. We have been a bit dismissive.'

'Yeah, Poppy's right, Dad. Hope would never run away. She's just making a point by shocking us into listening to her. Let's make her a nice vegan dinner,' Daisy said. 'We can have it ready for when she comes back. I bet she'll be back before it gets dark. She hates the dark.'

Joe clung to the twins' reasoning. Maybe Hope was just making a point. She did hate the dark. Maybe she would be back soon.

Six hours later, Joe paced up and down the kitchen as a pair of Guards, a man and a woman, asked him question after question.

What age is Hope? Hair colour? Length of hair? Weight? Eye colour? Height?

What was she wearing when she left the house?

Why would she run away?

Who was the last person to see her?

Why did she think they all hated her?

Why did they think she was trying to get to Sweden?

Why was she obsessed with Greta Thunberg?

Was she on social media?

What type of phone did she have?

The questions went on and on. Joe answered them as best he could, trying to stay calm and not think the worst. He had to believe Hope was OK. He had to believe they'd find her soon. But when they asked him if Hope had taken her passport and he had realised it was missing, his panic had worsened.

The twins sat side by side, crying. All thoughts of Hope just being dramatic were gone. It was almost ten p.m. and pitch-dark outside. They were now sick with worry about their sister. Seeing the Guards coming in and how stern they were about it all had apparently made them see how serious this was. Joe felt bad that they were so upset, but right now he had to focus on helping the police find Hope. Hope had left school eleven hours ago. She'd last spoken to Joe ten hours ago. Where *was* she? Was she on a plane? A boat? Was she scared? Was she safe?

The Guards were scribbling away in their little notebooks. Writing down all the details of Hope and her life. It was like a movie, except it wasn't: it was *Joe's* life and *Joe's* daughter.

Poppy was staring at the computer when she suddenly hopped up and went over to turn it on. She checked something, then turned around and shouted, 'Look! Hope's last Google search was "cheapest way to get from Dublin to Stockholm".' She clicked on the link. 'This is her travel plan. Quick, look.'

They all rushed over. There on the page was Hope's travel plan, clear for them all to see.

'Oh my God, she's on a boat on her own. Oh, Hope.' Joe felt sick. His baby girl was all alone out there on her way to another country.

'We'll find her, Joe. We have the travel details now, which makes it much easier to track her,' one of the Guards reassured him.

'It's OK, Dad.' Poppy rubbed his back while Daisy wiped his tears away with a soggy tissue that she had been crying into.

The Guards took down all the details of Hope's plan.

'We'll get on to our colleagues in Dublin Port and see if

177

we can get CCTV of her boarding. Then we'll contact the police in the UK and try to track her movements. If she made it onto the boat, she should be getting into Victoria Station in London in a couple of hours.' The female Guard looked at her watch.

'Don't worry, we'll have someone meet that bus and look after her,' her colleague assured them.

The two Guards stepped out of the room and began to make calls.

'Oh, thank God.' Joe gulped back tears. 'Well done again, Poppy.' He threw his arms around her.

'Yeah, well, don't forget *I'm* the one who came up with Greta's name and figured out that Hope was going to see her,' Daisy said, obviously feeling left out.

Joe pulled Daisy into a hug. 'I won't forget that, Daisy – thank you. All you girls are wonderful, and once we get Hope back I am never ever letting any of you out of my sight ever again. I'll be tracking you night and day.'

Daisy and Poppy pulled out of the hug and groaned.

'What?' Poppy exclaimed. 'Hang on, Dad. Just because Hope decides to run away and be all "Boo hoo, no one loves me because they won't turn the heating off and freeze to death" doesn't mean that Daisy and I need to get stalked by you!'

'It's my job to keep you girls safe, and I've failed with Hope. I will not fail again.'

They all turned as the two Guards came back into the room.

'Any news?' Joe asked.

The female Guard nodded. 'Hope was spotted on the boat and was seen boarding the bus, which is due to arrive in London soon.'

'Oh, thank God. Did you sort out for someone to meet the bus and protect her?' Joe asked.

'Yes, it's all organised. The bus will be met by two British Transport Police when it gets into Victoria Station at one-fifteen a.m. We'll have her home in no time, don't you worry.'

'The relief! I was so worried' Joe sobbed into his hands. The male Guard handed him a tissue.

'See, it's all OK, Dad, no need to freak out,' Daisy said.

'I'm going to put trackers on you all. I can't take the stress of this,' Joe said.

'Can you please tell our dad that it's not OK to start stalking us everywhere we go just because our little sister is a bit mad? We need freedom. We're fifteen.'

The male Guard smiled. 'I think your dad's right. I'm not advocating he puts trackers on you, but it is important for parents to know where their children are.'

'But not like, every second of every day,' Poppy exclaimed.

'We need to have a life.' Daisy looked concerned.

'Maybe give your poor dad a break here – he's worried about your sister. When we get her home, things will settle,' the Guard advised.

Joe wiped his eyes. 'Thank you so much for all your help. You must think I'm a terrible father, not knowing my child was so unhappy. Since my wife died, Hope has been a bit lost, and she became obsessed with Greta Thunberg and her environmental movement. Truth be told, I think we've all been a bit lost. I'm afraid I haven't been as supportive as I should have been of her passion for saving the planet. I tried to do as much as I felt was reasonable, but obviously she felt ... well ... very alone.' Joe wiped his eyes again with a tissue.

The twins leant in to hug him. 'You're not a terrible dad. A bit annoying sometimes, but not terrible,' Poppy said.

'We've been crappy sisters to Hope, we shouldn't have made fun of her,' Daisy admitted. 'This is not your fault. We're to blame. You've really tried since Mum died to be there for us,' she added, 'You're a great dad.'

'You three girls are my world,' Joe sobbed.

Poppy cried into Joe's shoulder. 'We love you, Dad. Everything is going to be OK.'

Joe wrapped his twin daughters into his arms and held on tight.

CHAPTER 23

Hope curled up in a ball in her window seat on the bus and tried to sleep. Her eyes ached with tiredness and her stomach rumbled. She was afraid to eat any more food. She only had two sandwiches and one chocolate bar left. She'd eaten everything else. She hadn't realised that travelling made you so hungry. All around her people were constantly eating and drinking and it made her want to eat too.

There was an air vent directly over her head that was blowing cold air on her. She was freezing. She pulled out her extra fleece and wrapped it around her neck and shoulders. It was midnight, way past her bedtime. Dad made her go to bed at nine thirty every weeknight.

But every time she tried to sleep, Hope would think about Dad, and how worried he'd be and how long her journey was and how she didn't know where Greta lived or where she was going …

Maybe it wouldn't be easy to find Greta in Stockholm. Maybe she was super private and no one knew where she lived. Maybe she'd freak out to find a stranger from Ireland on her doorstep. Maybe Greta's parents would chase Hope away. Maybe the twins were right – maybe Hope *was* a freak.

Hope rested her head against the window and cried silently. She was cold, hungry and scared. She wanted to go home. She wanted to call Dad and ask him to come and get her. But her phone was dead because she'd played games on the boat and run the battery down and she'd forgotten to pack her charger.

Hope's mind wouldn't stop whirring. She missed her bed. She missed her cosy duvet and pillow. She missed Dad and she even missed the twins a bit. Maybe this hadn't been such a good idea. She'd be in London in about two hours and then she still had to go on to Lille and Hamburg and then finally Stockholm. It seemed like a very long way.

An old woman had come up to Hope on the boat and asked her if she was on her own and if she was OK. Hope had pretended she was with a family who were sitting close by. She told the old lady that she was fighting with her brother, which was why she was sitting on her own. The woman had smiled and said, 'Oh, my children used to argue all the time too, but you know, pet, family is everything. No one will love you like your family. I hope you make up soon.'

She was right, Hope thought, family *was* everything. Hope had had a lot of time to think about things on this journey.

She knew her Dad loved her. He told her all the time. She didn't understand why he had said those mean things to Janice, but she had always known he loved her. But no one would ever love her the way Mum did. When Mum looked at her, she felt as if the sun was shining down on her. But Mum was gone, and Hope knew that she had to figure out a way to deal with life without her in it. The twins were really annoying, and they had each other, so she felt left out a lot, but they were nice to her sometimes. *Maybe*, Hope thought, *Dad's acting strangely because Mum's anniversary is coming up, and we are all hurting in our own way. People say stupid things when they're hurting. Maybe Dad didn't mean it, and maybe Rebecca had exaggerated the whole thing.* Hope felt like an idiot. She should have just talked to Dad instead of running away.

Hope sniffed the sleeve of her fleece. She'd sprayed some of Mum's perfume on it. 'Did I do the wrong thing, Mum?' Hope whispered to the dark night outside the bus window. 'Was I stupid? Am I going to be OK? I'm scared, Mum. I'm scared and I want to go home.' Silent tears ran down her face.

'Victoria Station,' a loud voice announced. 'Everyone off, this is Victoria Station.'

Hope opened her eyes. Around her, people were pulling bags down from the overhead baskets and pulling on their coats. They streamed out the door as she tried to wake up. She rubbed her eyes; it was pitch dark outside. Hope shivered. She went to pick up her backpack, but it was gone. She frantically looked around, on the seat, on the floor, but she couldn't see it anywhere. She looked at the seats on either side, but there was no sign of it. Someone must have stolen it while she was asleep. She began to cry. Her precious photos of Mum, the perfume ... it was all gone.

'Everyone off the bus!' the driver shouted.

Hope sobbed as she shuffled down the aisle. Her legs felt wobbly and her head felt woozy. She thought she was going to faint. What was she going to do? She just wanted

185

to go home. She slowly climbed down the steps of the bus, tears streaming down her face.

'Hope Dillon?'

Hope spun around. It was a policewoman. *Oh no.* Her heart began to race. There was another policewoman beside her, too. They looked very serious and scary.

'Are you Hope Dillon?' the woman asked again.

Hope didn't know what to do. Should she lie? It was bad to lie anyway, but to lie to a police officer was the worst. Police officers were trained to tell if you were lying. But how did they know her name and how did they know she would be here? Hope thought she must be in big trouble if the police were looking for her. She began to cry even harder.

'I'm sorry, I know I shouldn't have run away but ... but I just wanted to ... I'm just trying to ... I don't know ... I don't know what I want!' Hope sobbed. 'Am I going to go to prison? Are you going to lock me up in a cell?'

The police officer handed Hope a tissue. 'My name's Sarah, and this is my colleague, Penny. Your family are very worried about you, Hope. Running away is dangerous.'

'I know,' Hope said, still sobbing. 'I've been really scared and lonely. And I lost my backpack and my Mum's photos and ... I want to go home. Can I go home now? Is Dad furious with me?'

'He'll be very relieved to know that we've found you and that you're safe,' Sarah said.

Denise was talking into her phone. 'Yes, we have her here. She's fine. OK, will do.'

She turned to Hope. 'Right, Miss, you're coming back to the station with us. We'll get you some food and a warm blanket. Your dad is coming over on the first flight in the morning to get you and bring you home.'

'Is he? Really? My dad's coming?'

'Yes, he is.'

'He doesn't hate me?'

'Not at all. In fact, I think he loves you very, very much,' Sarah said.

Hope felt her body stop shaking. It was OK. Dad was coming to get her. She wasn't alone. She was safe, and she was going to be home soon. In her house, with her family, and she'd never leave them again.

CHAPTER 24

Hope snuggled up on a fold-out bed in the police station. She'd had a cup of hot chocolate and eaten a whole plate of biscuits. She was safe and warm. The police had found her backpack abandoned close to the bus. Her clothes and phone were gone but her mum's perfume and the two precious photos were still there. Hope held the photos close to her chest. She sprayed a small squirt of perfume onto her wrist and held it up to her nose. She felt her mother close to her. Hope finally let herself go, and she fell into a deep sleep.

She was dreaming about chocolate cake when she heard their voices outside the door.

'Hope! Where are you? I'm going to kill you!' Poppy shouted.

'Don't say that – she ran away because she thinks we don't understand her,' Daisy hissed.

'She ran away because she's obsessed with Greta and the planet.'

'No, Poppy, she ran away because she thinks we hate her. Remember the note?'

'Yeah, but she doesn't *really* think that, does she?' Poppy asked.

'I think your family has arrived.' Penny smiled down at Hope.

Hope threw back the blanket and jumped up. She ran to open the door.

Dad was charging down the corridor towards her. When he saw her, he stopped. His face crumpled up.

'Oh, Hope,' he cried.

He ran towards her and wrapped his big strong arms around her. Hope could feel his body shaking as he sobbed into her hair. It was the same way he had cried the day Mum died.

Hope had cried so much over the last day that she had no tears left. She patted Dad on the back. 'I'm so sorry, Dad. I'm sorry I ran away.'

Dad hugged her tighter. 'No, I'm the one that's sorry, Hope. I had no idea you felt so alone. I'm going to help you now, pet. I'm going to listen to you and try to be a better father. Your mum would never have let this happen.'

'You're a great dad. I'm sorry I worried you.'

'OK, enough apologising,' Poppy said. 'I want to hug her too.'

Dad pulled back and went to speak to the police officers.

Poppy hugged her little sister. 'Part of me wants to kill you for giving us all heart attacks, and just to be clear, I *do* find you annoying, but I don't hate you, Hope. I love you. I think you're a bit weird, but I still really really love you.'

'Me too,' Daisy said, pushing her way into the hug. 'You're our little sister – of course we love you. We don't understand you sometimes, but we love you.'

'Really?' Hope looked up at her older sisters.

'Yeah, totally,' Poppy said.

'You could be so much worse. Imagine if Rebecca was our little sister. Although we did see a different side to her last night.'

'Really? How?' Hope asked.

'When Dad called Janice to say you'd run away and asked if Rebecca had any idea where you were, Rebecca was really worried,' Daisy explained. 'She and Janice came straight over to the house, and Rebecca said you'd seemed really sad lately and she thought it was because you missed Mum – which shows she is human, after all, if she noticed that. Then, when the police said they'd found you in London, Rebecca offered to call her dad to get him to come and pick you up from the police station and bring you back to his mansion until we arrived to get you, but he didn't answer any of her calls. It was a bit embarrassing, actually. Rebecca kept calling and texting and he never replied.'

'Poor Rebecca. I think she's having a hard time. Her dad is all about his new wife and kid at the moment and ignoring her. I feel sorry for her,' Hope said.

'Don't feel *too* sorry for her; she's still really annoying,' Poppy said.

'Yeah, we heard her saying to Janice she couldn't believe how small our house is.' Daisy rolled her eyes.

'Speaking of Janice, your whole dramatic running away stint has broken Dad and her up,' Poppy told Hope.

'Yes!' Daisy grinned. 'Dad told Janice last night that he needs to focus on you and can't devote any time to her right now.'

Hope felt bad. She didn't want Dad to break up with Janice because of her – that wasn't fair.

She went over to Dad, who was talking to Sarah and Penny.

Hope tugged his arm, and he turned and smiled at her. He looked exhausted. 'Dad, please don't break up with Janice for me. I know you told her that I was a pain and driving you mad and that you want me to go to see a therapist. I'm sorry and I'll try not to go on so much about climate change.'

Dad looked confused. 'I never said anything of the sort to Janice. I don't think you're a pain, I'm really proud of you. I did tell her I was worried about you, and I did say that I was thinking about getting you to see a therapist to help you with your heartbreak over Mum, but that's it.'

'Oh.' Hope bit her lip. 'I heard Rebecca saying that you basically told Janice that you hated me.'

Dad shook his head. 'As If I would ever say that. I love every hair on your head and every bone in your body.' He hugged her again. 'And my friendship with Janice is over because it was never going anywhere. I had a nice time, but I want to focus on my family now. I want to be a better dad for all of you. Janice understands.'

'But I don't want you to be lonely. I want you to be happy.'

'I *am* happy, and I'm not lonely. I have my three girls.' Dad put his arms around his three daughters. 'We can spend more time together, and I'm not going to take my eyes off any of you again.'

'What?' Poppy clearly did not like the sound of that.

'Hang on a minute,' Daisy said.

Just then, Penny called Dad over to sign some forms.

'This is all your fault,' Poppy hissed at Hope.

'Now Dad is never going to let us go out. We need to get him back with Janice ASAP.' Daisy chewed her thumbnail.

'You're going to have to become friends with Rebecca,' Poppy told Hope.

'Yeah, best friends,' Daisy agreed.

'No way.' Hope wasn't doing that. Rebecca might have shown a nicer side to her personality, but they were never going to be mates.

Poppy glared at her. 'You broke them up, so you have to fix it.'

'We all wanted them to break up,' Hope reminded her.

'Yeah, well, that was before you ran away and Dad said he was going to start watching us twenty-four-seven. We need him to have a distraction and Janice is a distraction.'

'I'll think of another way,' Hope said.

'You'd better – and quickly. We want to go to Harry Considine's party next week,' Daisy said.

Hope nodded. 'OK, I'll try, but can you give me a break? I've had a really hard few days.'

Daisy and Poppy stared at her. 'So have we, Hope,' Daisy pointed out. 'We haven't slept a wink. We were sick with worry. It was Poppy who found out where you were going – she did a Google search history. So you need to thank her for basically saving your life.'

'Thanks, Poppy,' Hope said.

Poppy gave her twin some credit. 'Daisy figured out that the "only other person who understands you" was Greta Thunberg.'

'Thanks, Daisy, that was smart.'

'Dad gave us a big lecture on the plane over this morning – do not freak out about the plane, I know you'd probably have preferred if we'd rowed over, but we were so dying to see you that we had to get here as fast as possible.'

'It's OK.' Hope smiled. She was happy to let it go: it had meant they'd got to her quickly, and she needed them, more than she'd ever realised.

'Anyway, Dad lectured us about how we have to be nicer to you and help out with your save the climate crusade. We will, we promise, but you have to relax on the no flushing the loo and the two-minute showers, OK?'

'Yeah, take it slow, Hope,' Poppy agreed. 'We want to help, we really do, but you have to ease us into it.'

'And I want the money you stole from me back,' Daisy added firmly.

'Me too,' said Poppy. 'That was not cool.'

Hope fished in her pocket and handed them back their money. 'I only used my money in the end. I was going to use yours today to buy the tickets from here to Stockholm.'

The twins took their money back.

'I'm sorry I took it. I know it was wrong.'

Poppy took her sister's hand. 'Hey, Hope, how about we go to Bershka, and Daisy and I treat you to some cool clothes? It can be a kind of "welcome home" and early Christmas present.'

'Really?'

'Yes, we want to spoil you,' Daisy said.

'We know that you're hurting a lot right now with Mum's anniversary in two days. We're all hurting,' Poppy told her.

Hope fought back tears, 'It's just so hard. When does it get easier?' she asked.

Poppy shrugged. 'I dunno, I think we just have to keep on going, and one day the pain won't be so bad.'

'Would it help if we talked about her more?' Daisy asked

Hope nodded. 'Yes, I think so.'

'OK, we'll do that then,' Daisy said.

'But not right now. I can't take any more emotion this morning. Can we please go shopping now?' Poppy asked.

Hope took a deep breath. 'OK, don't freak out, but I'd prefer to go to an eco-friendly clothes shop. I heard there's a really good one near Covent Garden, where the clothes are made from sustainable, organic and recycled materials.'

The twins rolled their eyes. 'OK, fine,' Daisy said. 'We'll take you there. Happy now?'

Hope grinned. 'Yes, very.'

Each twin put an arm around their little sister and they walked out of the police station, chatting and laughing together. Dad followed them, beaming from ear to ear.

Hope looked up at the bright blue sky. 'I'm going to be OK, Mum. It's all going to be OK from now on.'

CHAPTER 25

ope tiptoed downstairs to get everything ready. She turned on the Christmas tree lights and the gas fire in the TV room to make it cosy. She pulled her gifts out of the straw bag she had hidden them in and placed them under the tree. Then she put on some Christmas music and lit the big red candles on the mantlepiece.

She sat warming her toes by the dancing fire and looked at the angel on top of the tree.

'Happy Christmas, Mum,' she whispered. 'I wish you were here. I miss you so much. But I know you're with us in our hearts, always.'

The door burst open and the twins came tumbling in, wearing matching Christmas reindeer onesies.

Dad followed them, carrying a cup of coffee.

'Oh my God, it's a Christmas miracle!' Poppy said. 'Hope has put the fire on!'

Hope laughed. 'I reckon it's OK on special days.'

'Right, pressies,' Daisy said, clapping her hands.

The twins reminded Hope that they had already bought her Christmas presents in London a few weeks earlier.

'But, even though we treated you then, we do have one small extra present for you.' Poppy handed Hope a gift. 'And, as you can see, we were all recycling-friendly and wrapped it in newspaper, so we didn't use any new wrapping paper,' she added.

Hope opened it – it was a framed certificate. She looked closer. There was a picture of a cow doing a poo. Across the top of the certificate, it read, '*The Gift of Poo.*' Underneath was written, '*Happy Christmas, Hope. We have donated €20 to poo.*'

Dad leant over Hope's shoulder as the twins cracked up laughing. 'What is this? Are you making fun of Hope?' He glared at them.

'NO! It's for real.' Poppy giggled.

'We found it on the internet. It's some kind of environmental organisation that turns poo into compost,'

Daisy explained through snorts of laughter.

'Look.' Poppy pointed to the small print on the certificate. '*This planet-saving gift will improve the quality of life of local farming communities.*'

'You see, it's a proper environmental do-gooder present for Hope – but it's also kind of hilarious.' Daisy chuckled.

Hope grinned. 'I love it. When my friends ask what my sisters got me for Christmas, I'll say a big pile of poo.' They all cracked up; even Dad saw the funny side.

The twins then opened their present from Dad, which was tickets to go to see Harry Styles in concert. They jumped on top of Dad, squashing him with their joy.

While the twins were showing their appreciation to Dad, Hope went to the tree and fetched her presents for them. She handed the twins one package each and then another to Dad. They were small and wrapped in newspaper.

The twins started ripping theirs open. 'I bet it's a Save the Ocean T-shirt,' Daisy said.

'Or a set of bamboo toothbrushes.' Poppy giggled.

'Oh ...' they whispered as the paper fell away from the gifts. 'Oh, Hope.'

'It's beautiful.' Poppy's voice wobbled.

'It's perfect.' Daisy wiped a tear from her eye.

Dad looked up; the twins were each holding a framed photo of Mum with her arms around them. The picture was of her and the twins standing on the beach, the sun setting behind them. The three of them were laughing. The photo showed a moment of pure joy.

'Oh, Hope, that's so thoughtful,' Dad said.

He pulled the paper from his gift and stared down at it. Silence.

Hope held her breath. Maybe it had been the wrong thing to do. Maybe she had made a big mistake.

Dad looked up, tears in his eyes. 'It's the best present ever. Thank you.'

The twins moved over to see what Hope had given him. Dad was holding a framed photo of himself and the twins and Hope standing in front of the Christmas tree two years ago. Mum had taken the photo. Hope had printed, *'You'll never walk alone'* across the top of it.

'I know I'm never alone with you three,' said Dad. 'Thanks for reminding me of that, Hope.'

'OK, Hope gets the prize for best gifts this year,' Poppy said.

'I dunno, I still think the Gift of Poo is genius.' Daisy winked at Hope.

They gathered up the paper to put in the recycling bin. Hope was wondering if maybe Dad had forgotten her, or maybe didn't have any money left to buy her anything after she'd cost the family so much when they'd all had to fly to London to find her. But then Dad said he had one more gift.

'I tried to think of something really special for you, Hope. The twins helped me figure out the best thing to give you. We hope you like it.'

'It's not more poo,' Poppy assured her.

Hope opened the small package. It was an envelope. Inside was a ticket to a climate-change conference in London with guest speakers including ...

GRETA THUNBERG!!!

'Oh Dad,' she said, gulping back tears. 'Oh my gosh, is this for real? Seriously? Am I going to see her?'

Dad hugged her. 'Yes. You and I are going to the conference in three weeks' time.'

Hope covered her face with her hands and sobbed. She was going to see Greta in real life. She was going to hear her speak. She was actually going to be in the same room as her. Wow wow wow. This was the best present ever. 'Thank you thank you thank you thank you thank you!' Hope threw her arms around Dad's neck.

Dad held her tight. 'You deserve it, Hope – you're a wonderful girl and I'm so proud of you and what you're trying to do to help save our planet.'

Hope then went over to the twins to hug them. 'Thank you too,' she said.

Poppy leant down to whisper in her ear. 'The best part is that while Dad is taking you to that snoring boring conference, we'll have a free house!'

'Finally, your climate-change stuff is actually making our lives better.' Daisy grinned.

Hope looked up at the Christmas tree angel and smiled. There was still a big hole where Mum should be, but the pain was getting a little easier to bear and their broken family was coming closer together, finding hope, looking after each other and being kinder to one another. Mum would be proud.

And in three weeks Hope was going to see Greta Thunberg in person and hear more about how she could save the planet.

She couldn't wait!

Acknowledgements

I wrote this book so that all children can understand that one person *can* make a difference to the world. You are the children that will have to clean up the mess that we – your parents – have made of the planet. You are the generation that are going to save the environment and put the climate crisis at the top of your priority list.

A big thank you ...

To Greta Thunberg for being such a courageous, brave and brilliant role model for young people.

To my skilled editor, Venetia Gosling.

To my dedicated publicist, Fiona Murphy.

To my fantastic agent, Marianne Gunn O'Connor.

To all the team at Gill Publishing, who have been so fantastic to work with and who are so passionate about getting books out into the world.

To my three children, Hugo, Geordy and Amy, who I love (and nag) so much!

To Troy for supporting me and cheering me on all the way.

To my Mum, my sister and my brother. I was lucky enough to grow up in a lovely home full of books and learned to love reading from an early age. I have tried to pass that on to my kids.

To my friends, who always make me laugh and remember to have fun in life.

To my two cats, Minnie and Luna, who come and purr or grunt (Minnie can't purr, she grunts) on my lap when I'm writing.

Most of all, I want to thank you, my readers. I love writing stories about things that really matter and I hope you enjoy reading them too. Keep reading books, they make you smart and interesting. Finally, remember this – you can make a difference, so be brave and fearless.